"I thought your own c

as she walk

"Coffee?

"Please." Duane smiled. "I'd be a fool to eat my cooking when you've got the café here."

Linda smiled back.

Duane told himself that smiling was a good beginning for the two of them. That's where they'd started back in junior high school.

"I'm sorry I've been gone."

Linda looked at him cautiously.

"You needed your friends, and I wasn't here."

"It's okay," Linda said softly as she pulled out her order pad. "What'll it be?"

Duane resisted the impulse to throw his heart at her feet. "Scrambled eggs and toast."

Books by Janet Tronstad

Love Inspired

*Dry Creek

JANET TRONSTAD

grew up on a small farm in central Montana. One of her favorite things to do was to visit her grandfather's bookshelves, where he had a large collection of Zane Grey novels. She's always loved a good story. Today Janet lives in Pasadena, California, where she is a full-time writer.

Dry Creek Sweethearts
Janet Tronstad

Steeple
Hill®

Published by Steeple Hill Books™

STEEPLE HILL BOOKS

Steeple
Hill®

ISBN-13: 978-0-373-87475-0
ISBN-10:   0-373-87475-8

DRY CREEK SWEETHEARTS

Copyright © 2008 by Janet Tronstad

Printed in U.S.A.

And we know that all things work together for good to them that love God, to them who are the called according to his purpose.

—*Romans* 8:28

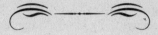

This book is dedicated with love to my brother-in-law, Duane Enger. He has graciously allowed me to use his name for the hero in this book with the understanding that I would also include his dog, Boots. Boots plays himself in the book, but the only thing my Duane has in common with his namesake in this book is his love for his high school sweetheart, my sister, Margaret. Well, that and his affection for an old Silverton guitar that he sometimes brings out to play in the evenings.

Chapter One

"I don't care if he *did* grow up in Dry Creek, he's still not one of us. Not anymore." Linda Morgan struggled to keep her voice neutral as she flipped the sign in her café window to Closed and began to stack chairs on tables so she could mop the floor.

A neutral calm was the best she could expect of herself when it came to Duane Enger.

She should have refused to let her younger sister, Lucy, hang his old guitar on the wall of the café when the idea first came up months ago. Then she and her sister wouldn't even be having this conversation now.

Lucy was too young to know there was no point in building a shrine to someone who had left everything behind so he could go off and chase his dream of becoming a rock star. Every time Linda looked at the guitar she remembered that the old six-string Silvertone hadn't been good enough for Duane to take with him. The frets were worn down and it needed new strings. So he had left the Silvertone behind, just as he'd eventually left everything and everyone behind, even her.

The small Montana town of Dry Creek had not been big enough for Duane and his dreams.

Of course, Linda couldn't tell her sister all of this—especially not in the tone of voice she was using in her head as she thought it. Lucy had a tender heart and Linda didn't want her to worry that anyone around here held anything against the man Lucy had just started to idolize. A teenage girl needed heroes, and Duane was better than most who were out there.

Besides, Linda told herself, the whole thing with Duane shouldn't bother her anymore. Lots of people were disappointed by their high school sweethearts. She wasn't the only one. It wasn't even worth talking about. It had been eight long years since Duane left Dry Creek. That was plenty of time for a broken heart to heal.

Right now, Linda had more important things to worry about anyway, like keeping the floor clean after all the rain they'd had this week. The road into Dry Creek was asphalt, but the parking area in front of her café was pure dirt. That meant mud and lots of it. She'd already mopped the floor twice today and she had to do it again tonight before she and Lucy headed home. A woman who needed to mop a floor that often didn't have time to be thinking about some man who had left her behind to pursue his fantasy of stardom.

Linda lifted the last chair up. It was half her fault anyway. She never should have trusted a man who couldn't even stick with the name he was given the day he was born. Duane had traded his name for a stage name before he left Dry Creek. That should have been her first clue about how much commitment the man had in his bones. He eventually started going by Duane again, but lots of people still knew him as the Jazz Man.

Linda set the chair down hard on the table and winced when she heard the soft slam. Okay, so Duane might still bother her a little more than she would like. Which was probably natural; she was only human. She might have grown closer to God since Duane left, but she still had a way to go. Her heart had healed, but her head still hadn't totally forgiven him or herself for believing in him.

Linda thought Lucy had given up the argument until she saw her sister looking at her with reproach in her eyes.

"But we have to display these things. He's famous." Lucy held up the letter she'd framed to hang beside the guitar and gazed at it as if it were written in pure gold. "The Jazz Man is the only famous person to ever come out of Dry Creek—right here—and he *remembers* us."

The Jazz Man is what Duane had started calling himself just before he left. All through high school, he'd played and sung his own arrangements, along with songs from the old jazz masters like Duke Ellington. Linda had sung with him, especially on the classics. Back then, Duane had been happy enough with himself and his jazz revival plans.

Then, he set his eyes on Hollywood and nothing was good enough, not his name, not his guitar, not his friends. Not even his hometown.

Still, Linda told herself, none of that was Lucy's fault. Besides, if Linda let her sister hang the letter on the wall as she'd been requesting, it might actually help them both forget about the piece of paper since it would no longer be in her sister's pocket where she could pull it out and read it every ten seconds.

"Go ahead and put your letter up there if you want." Linda tried to sound gracious. "But, just so you know, he's not that famous. There are lots of places where people haven't even heard of him."

Like Timbuktu. And maybe that nursing home in Miles City. The more Linda thought about it the more she knew she was overreacting. Lucy might have been carrying that letter around with her since it came in the mail a week ago. And she might have gone all dewy-eyed every time she read it. But it was the memories that it brought back to Linda that were the problem, not the letter itself.

Linda suspected she'd worn a very similar look on her face when she was four years younger than Lucy and had seen Duane for the first time. At the age of eleven, he had come to Dry Creek to live in the Enger family home on the outskirts of town. Rumor had it that Duane had been arrested trying to steal a car in Chicago and the courts had sent him to Dry Creek to get reformed under the stern guidance of his great-aunt, Cornelia Enger.

To Linda back then, Duane had looked every bit the tough city boy people said he was. He wore ragged black sneakers when the rest of the boys in school were wearing leather cowboy boots. And he had that old Silvertone guitar strapped to his back all the time. It was whispered that he knew how to hot-wire a car, pass a fake twenty-dollar bill and French-kiss a girl. No one was quite sure if the latter knowledge came from experience or observation, but the adults didn't like it no matter how he'd learned about it.

Linda's mother asked her not to talk to Duane in school and that had made Linda determined to be his friend. The adults in Dry Creek all eyed the boy cautiously, but Linda decided he just looked lonely. He scowled at everyone, but Linda just kept smiling at him until one day, when they were in the seventh grade, he smiled back.

It wasn't much of a smile, but the thaw had begun. Eventually, he would play a song on his guitar for her now and then. Over time, he seemed to fall in love with Linda as much as she was with him. She was thrilled when they were freshmen in high school and he said she was his girl, and then when they were sophomores and he called her his sweetheart. When they were eighteen, he secretly asked her to marry him…someday when everything was good…someday when he could support them…someday when his dreams had had a chance to come true.

Of course, someday never came.

"It's just as well he left Dry Creek," Linda finally said. "He would never have been happy here."

She didn't know what would have made Duane happy. Back then, she had thought it was his music. He'd learned to play the guitar from some man in Chicago and Duane had been fierce about wanting to spark another major jazz revival. Linda believed he could bend the whole music world to his thinking by the sheer force of his wanting to make it happen. As it turned out, her belief lasted longer than his determination. He gave up on jazz and joined a rock band that promised a quicker route to fame. Duane was impatient with everything. He hated lines and contracts and waiting for people to respond to his music.

So, he left jazz and went to where the music beat faster. The rock band he joined toured and recorded and, now and then, even had a song with a few jazz overtones in it. She knew those jazz moments came from Duane.

Not that Linda really listened to the songs from Duane's band anymore. If she heard something from them come on the radio, she turned it off. She didn't want to be wondering what the words to these songs meant. Or, if Duane had written them and who he had in mind when he wrote them. Or if he ever sang the songs he had written for her. Or if he even thought about her anymore.

Not that she wanted Duane to think about her now. It was much too late for that. And it was okay. God's plan had been for her to be in Dry Creek. It was her place; hers and Lucy's. When their mother died and left them alone, the people of Dry Creek had made a circle around them and became their family. She and her sister wouldn't have been happy anyplace else. And she was happy here. Really, she was.

Sometimes her memories of Duane seemed like nothing more than a long-ago dream, vaguely sweet but irrelevant to her life today.

"I doubt he even signs those letters himself." Linda brought herself back to Lucy and the problem at hand. So much had changed. "He probably has someone who does the whole thing for him. You could have been anybody writing to him and you would have gotten the same letter back."

She hoped she wasn't being too hard on her sister. She hadn't known Lucy had sent a letter telling Duane all about the outdoor concert she and the other high school students had given last spring, until Lucy got a letter in response. Linda would have protested if she'd known Lucy had written; her sister didn't need to waste her time thinking about someone who wasn't giving anyone in Dry Creek a moment's thought.

"He signed it 'Love, Duane.' That has to mean something."

Obviously, Linda thought, her skepticism wasn't making a dent in Lucy's adoration.

"It means he hopes we buy his new CD." Linda stepped over so she could take a closer look at the letter her sister held. "I don't even know if that's his real signature."

There was a time when Linda would have definitely recognized Duane's handwriting, but eight years was a long time and she'd had better things to think about. She had a business to run and, after her mother had died, she had a younger sister to raise. Besides, Duane had probably changed the way he signed his name many times over the years anyway. Change seemed to be his pattern.

"But you two used to be friends," Lucy protested. "I remember all those times when he snuck out to the farm when Mom was at work. He was your *boyfriend*. I saw him kiss you dozens of times."

Linda felt her whole face stiffen. Duane had been more than her boyfriend; she'd said yes when he'd asked her to marry him someday. She'd been foolish enough to think that meant she was his fiancée and she'd waited for him like a woman of her word until she visited him and it became apparent things would never work out.

Not that she was going to tell Lucy that. No one needed to know about her empty dreams. "Things change."

With Duane, things had really changed.

Everything was gone. Duane's great-aunt had died in her sleep just after he graduated from high school. She'd been ill for some time and the doctor said she'd just hung on until she could see Duane through school. Linda had stood with Duane as they buried his aunt and she'd felt him tremble.

There were no Engers in Dry Creek now, except for Duane's old dog, Boots. Duane had taken Boots with him when he first left Dry Creek and then, a year or so later, he'd asked Mrs. Hargrove if Boots could live with her for a while. He paid the older woman, of course, but still that didn't make it right.

A dog should be with its master, especially this dog. Boots would *die* for Duane.

Every time Linda thought about it she was indignant on Boots's behalf. Duane couldn't help it when he lost his great-aunt, but he didn't need to lose Boots, too. Besides, a man shouldn't ignore the kind of loyalty Boots had. It should count for something more than just remembering to send a check to cover some dog biscuits. And, if the truth were told, Linda wasn't even sure Duane sent the checks regularly. Maybe he'd completely forgotten about the dog.

Mrs. Hargrove was too kind to evict Boots even if she never received a dime for his care. Now that she thought of it, Linda wondered if Duane had some purebred show dog in Hollywood that he used for publicity shots. Maybe he'd replaced Boots just the way he'd replaced everyone else.

Linda almost said something, but Lucy clearly wasn't thinking about the injustice befalling anyone left behind in Dry Creek. She was looking straight at Linda with a hopeful look on her face.

"You went to Hollywood to visit him," Lucy said softly. "Remember? I stayed with Mrs. Hargrove and you went to see him. That had to mean something."

"That was a long time ago."

It was shortly after their mother had died. Their father had been dead for years by then and their mother's death left Linda broken. It was too much. She had gone to see Duane as instinctively as she'd wept at her mother's graveside. He'd opened his arms to her, too. She'd been comforted until she realized he had no intention of returning to Dry Creek and she couldn't go with him on the road chasing his dreams as he'd asked, not when she suddenly had a seven-year-old sister to think about. So she'd left him a note saying things just wouldn't work out between them and she had come back to Dry Creek.

Duane had brought Boots back shortly after that, but Linda had refused to see Duane then. She needed to get on with her life and she couldn't do that if Duane kept stopping by. At the time, she hadn't known it would be Duane's last visit to the town. His great-aunt had left him her house, and Linda had thought Duane would need to stop by to tend it. It was his duty to take care of that house; she thought he'd be back often. But he wasn't.

"I still think we should name the café after him. We could be The Jazz Café in memory of him," Lucy said.

"We don't need a name. We're the only café in Dry Creek."

Dry Creek had a hardware store, a café, and a part-time bakery. That and a dozen or so houses were all that was around, except for the church, of course. The church was the heart of the community. But the café was central, too. No one even needed directions to the café. It was right there for everyone to see. Linda had never worried about having any signs up except the Open and Closed one in the big front window.

"I bet people will pay more to eat in a place with a name," Lucy said. "Don't you think?"

"I'm not going to charge more just because there's a name over the door. Besides, the food tastes the same whether or not we call ourselves something."

"Lance says we need a name. That it will increase business."

Linda sighed at that. Besides her, the only other friend Duane had in high school had been Lance Walker, a boy who was part Sioux and had come off the Pine Ridge reservation in South Dakota with a chip on his shoulder that rivaled Duane's. The two were competitive with each other about everything, but they had become firm friends.

Lance had been sent to Dry Creek to live with a distant relative, Mr. Higgins, just as Duane had been sent to live with his great-aunt. Lance didn't have Duane's wanderlust, though. He'd stayed in the area after high school, and now he rode rodeo in Miles City. After he'd won a couple of events, he'd begun looking for sponsors for the shirt he wore on his back. Linda had offered to sponsor him even if she didn't have a name to advertise on the shirt, but he refused, saying he was taking advertising not charity.

"Everything isn't always about dollars and cents," Linda said. "Lance knows that."

Lance had his pride, and Linda had begun to wonder if he was serious when he kept asking her to close the café early some Saturday night so she could go to dinner with him in Miles City. At first, she thought he was asking her out because of old times, but she was no longer sure. She wished she could feel half the emotions about Lance as she did about Duane's old dog, Boots.

Linda told herself she didn't want to wind up some disappointed old woman who was still bitter because her first love had left her a million years ago and she'd never moved on. Anyway, it would be good to date again. She could hardly use the excuse of raising Lucy much longer, especially now that her sister was a sophomore in high school.

Linda used to love to date. When she was Lucy's age, she had her hair streaked with red and her mascara loaded with glitter. She and Duane used to drive into Miles City every Saturday night just to go line dancing. Sometimes Lance would go along with them and the three of them bumped shoulders with strangers and gave wild coyote yells when the line broke apart. It was more aerobic exercise than dancing really, but they liked the feet-stomping excitement of it. They'd wind down with a soda or malt at a late-night diner. Duane liked strawberry. She chose vanilla.

Those days seemed like an eternity ago. Linda couldn't recall when she had first started feeling like such an old woman. She was only twenty-seven years old and some days she'd rather spend the evening with her feet propped up than go anywhere. Maybe she needed some new vitamins.

Of course, she had plenty of energy during the day; it was just when she thought of dating that she got tired and wanted to stay home in her old bathrobe and watch television.

"Mama always told us to let our light shine," Lucy said softly. "I think she'd want you to give the café a nice name."

Linda's eyes softened as she looked over at her sister. Lucy was carefully marking a place on the wall to put a nail so she could hang her framed letter. Lucy didn't really remember their mother saying that about their light; she remembered Linda telling her that their mother had said something like that.

Their mother hadn't said much about love or happiness or anything that a young girl could hold on to so Linda added a few quotes of her own to the stories she told Lucy on the theory that their mother might have said something like that if she'd given her and Lucy more than a passing thought. Her mother had been so caught up in mourning the death of their father years ago that she hadn't paid much attention to either of her two daughters. The admonition to stay away from Duane Enger was the only advice her mother had ever given her about men.

Linda knew a young girl needed more than that. She needed to feel loved. She also needed to have some words to guide her. And someone to listen to her and understand what she was saying.

"Maybe you're right," Linda finally said. "A name for the café couldn't hurt us."

Lucy smiled up at her. "You won't be sorry."

"Just think of something without Jazz in it. All we need is a simple name. Something like the Morgan Café or the Sunshine or—"

"Definitely not the Sunshine Café," Lucy said. "Not in this mud."

The rain was a blessing in this part of Southern Montana. For years, there hadn't been enough of it and the ranchers had been worried about drought. Now the skies were being overly generous with moisture, which made a lot of people, and their cattle, happy even if it didn't do much for the floor of Linda's café.

Still, Linda knew that happy ranchers made good customers, so she thanked God for the rain.

"We'll think of a name on the way home, after I finish mopping." Linda congratulated herself on moving Lucy's attention away from the letter. Hopefully, once it was hanging on the wall, Lucy would forget about it.

Linda pulled her mop out of the bucket. The lemon smell of her cleaning solution cut through the old coffee smell. Linda prided herself on her black-and-white floor. That, along with the gray Formica-topped tables, gave the whole place a fifties look. And it was neat and orderly, just the way she liked. She had an old malt machine on the counter and two-dozen malt glasses hanging from a rack above it. She was also saving up for a genuine ruby-red jukebox to put next to the door of the kitchen. When that happened, everything would be perfect.

And, if the decor wasn't enough to inspire a name, the café itself should be. She made an honest cup of coffee and charged fair prices. She ran a working person's café that offered good value. There should be a name in all of that somewhere.

"The name shouldn't be too froufrou, though," Linda told her sister. "Remember who most of our customers are. Ranching families. We could just call ourselves the Dry Creek Café and everyone would be happy."

Lucy wasn't listening. "I should write and tell the Jazz Man about his guitar hanging on our wall." Lucy adjusted the framed letter she'd just hung. "I think he'd want to know, especially if we have a name."

Linda sighed. Maybe she'd made a mistake in letting Lucy think life was filled with more love floating around than it really was. "He gets lots of letters, honey. Tons of them probably."

"But not letters from Dry Creek," Lucy said confidently. "This is his home. He wants to hear from us."

Linda didn't answer. What could she say? So she just pushed her mop across the floor. The rain was coming down steady still. She'd just seen a flash of lightning and she wanted to get the floor mopped quickly so they could get back to the farm before the roads got any worse. She didn't want to get stuck in the mud.

"I think he might want to know about all the rain we've had this spring," Lucy continued. "He knows how dry it usually is so he'll be happy. His great-aunt's lilac bushes are going to be in full bloom pretty soon if the rain ever stops."

A person had to drive past the Enger driveway in order to take the road out to the Morgan farm. It always made Linda sad to see the old Enger house standing there without anyone living in it, so she tried not to look in that direction as she passed.

It was time to stop avoiding things, she decided. She needed to put the past to rest.

She might just stop someday soon at the wide place where the Enger driveway met the main road and that old bent stop sign stood. The lilac bushes lined the driveway to the house and the fragrance of those blossoms would be worth taking a few minutes to stop and admire. She and Duane had shared a kiss or two, parked in the driveway and smelling those lilacs. Maybe it would be therapeutic for her to face those lilacs again by herself and say a final goodbye to her memories of Duane.

After all, the two people who had crashed into that stop sign twenty-some years ago, and bent it to the crooked heart shape it was today, had found peace last year by facing the ghosts of their past. They'd hit the stop sign while trying to elope to Las Vegas and it took them both coming back to the sign to figure out that they still wanted to be together.

Of course, things were different with her and Duane. They wouldn't come together again. When she smelled those lilac bushes in the Enger driveway, she would be alone. Still, maybe she'd find some peace and be able to move on and love someone else. She sighed; it was time.

"Everybody misses their home," Lucy said firmly as Linda put her mop in a corner and gathered up their jackets.

"Like I said earlier, Dry Creek isn't Duane's home anymore." Linda gave Lucy her jacket. "He lives in Hollywood. You know that."

Duane could be living on the moon; he was so distant.

Linda put her jacket on and opened the door going out of the café. A burst of cold, damp air came inside.

"Home is where the heart is," Lucy said as she stepped out on the porch. She waited under the overhang so she wouldn't get wet. "Mama used to tell us that. Remember?"

There was another flash of lightning in the distance.

Linda wished she hadn't relied quite so much on clichés when she was inventing the stories for Lucy about what their mother had said. Linda turned the light off and shut the door behind her as she closed the café for the night.

"That might be a customer coming," Lucy said as she looked down the road entering Dry Creek and pointed. "There's a set of headlights."

The rain was heavy and the night was black, but the lights were visible even though they were blurred.

Linda saw them. "The headlights are high. It's probably a cattle truck going out to the Elkton Ranch. But don't worry about it. Those ranch hands always carry a thermos of coffee. Besides, they won't want to stop for anything at this time of night, especially if they have animals in the back. Once the thunder gets closer, it'll spook anything in the truck so they want to get home and unloaded as soon as they can."

Lucy nodded. "Maybe it's Lance."

Linda shrugged. "Could be."

Lance periodically worked for the Elkton Ranch when they needed extra help or he needed extra income.

The sisters both walked quickly to Linda's old car. Fortunately, the vehicle started right up. Linda backed the car out of its parking space and drove down the asphalt road to the gravel road leading to the Morgan family farm.

It was too bad she and Lucy were traveling in the same direction as that old cattle truck, Linda thought, because that meant they wouldn't be passing it. Even if Lance wasn't in the cab of the truck, the other ranch hands were always good for a big wave, especially on a stormy night like tonight. Linda could use some down-to-earth men to cheer her up. Thankfully, not every man around here needed to be a big star to be happy.

There was really something to be said for a man like Lance, Linda told herself. He was content just pulling a good horse to ride in the annual Bucking Horse Sale, a rodeo in Miles City, and working cattle at the Elkton Ranch. There was nothing in Lance that yearned for something bigger than what he already had. He'd be happy to stay in Dry Creek forever. He'd make someone a good solid husband.

Linda wondered if Duane's dreams had made him happy over the years. He had loved to play his jazz music for people. Now, instead of an audience of twenty, the size he'd had on a good day in Dry Creek, he played for thousands of fans at the same time. The sound of the music might be different and rock music might not be his first choice, but he was probably very pleased with himself.

After all, he was on the radio, which was more than she could say for anyone else who had grown up around here, including Lance with his local rodeo fame. It was certainly more than she could say for herself.

Yes, she decided, Duane Enger probably was very happy.

Chapter Two

Duane Enger was miserable and sick and tired.

Everything was dark outside the bus except for the shine of the headlights on the wet asphalt as he drove into Dry Creek. He saw the taillights of a car in the distance so he knew he wasn't the only one unfortunate enough to be driving around in the heavy rain. He figured his manager, Phil, who was sitting in the passenger seat right behind him, had seen the lights, too.

"There were people in that car," Phil muttered as he leaned forward to complain in Duane's ear. "And you let them get away."

Phil had been driving like a maniac on the way up here, refusing to let any cars pass them. Duane had finally concluded the man might be having a midlife crisis even though he was only thirty-six. Of course, it had also occurred to Duane that Phil might have been lying about his age since the day they'd met. No one wanted to be old in the music business, especially in the teenage market.

Phil was short and pudgy so he looked as if he could be any age. He was completely bald so he didn't even have any hair to turn gray. Not that the man's age mattered, in Duane's opinion, unless it affected how he acted behind the wheel.

For most of the trip, Duane had been too sick to pay any attention to what was happening outside the bus. But he had stopped dozing in Idaho when Phil ran a stop sign and, once they hit Miles City, Duane asked to take over the driving. There weren't enough road signs to clearly mark the way to Dry Creek so Phil reluctantly agreed Duane could drive.

That didn't stop Phil from scooting forward on the seat behind the driver's seat and giving Duane his constant opinions on everything, especially the other cars on the road.

Duane hunched over the steering wheel and coughed. "Not—"

His voice cracked.

Phil held out a cup of the coffee they'd bought an hour ago at a gas station in Miles City. "I keep saying you need to be resting your voice. I know the doctor said it was not a virus, but he meant for you to *rest your voice*."

"I can talk." Duane did his best, but the words came out thin as he reached out with one hand and took the cup.

The other man didn't even answer. The windshield wipers were on full speed and the rain beat on the roof of the bus. Duane took two gulps of the lukewarm coffee and handed the cup back to Phil.

"I thought when you said you wanted to go home that

there would at least be a clinic around here. You know, for emergencies. Like pneumonia," Phil said.

"Don't have pneumonia," Duane whispered, almost sure that he was right. He'd had a low-grade fever that seemed to come and go, but that was probably nothing.

"I don't even see a sign for a veterinarian. Those cows we passed must get sick sometimes."

"Doc Norris. Edge of town."

Phil grunted. "At least we could have radioed ahead for a people doctor to meet us in Ensenada if you'd followed the plan and gone on that yacht like you were supposed to. That yacht had everything."

Phil was big on plans and yachts.

"Reporters—" Duane's voice went to a high squeak, but he thought he made his point. Just to be sure, he added in a whisper, "With me coughing and sneezing like some typhoid case."

Phil put his hand on Duane's shoulder. "Let's take it easy. I know the doctor in Los Angeles said it was probably just vocal strain and a sinus infection. But what if he's wrong?"

"Not wrong." Duane hoped he was right. "Specialist."

Two days ago, Duane and Phil had been parked at the San Pedro pier south of Los Angeles, all set to join the rest of the band members on a private yacht heading down the Mexican Riviera to Puerto Vallarta. The yacht was supposed to get them some attention in the emerging markets south of the border. No one had seen the sales reports from their last CD yet, but they were likely to be discouraging and Phil's plan was to get the band solidly in front of the Latin market before the U.S.

market started to shrink. The band members were supposed to look like the carefree successful young musicians everyone thought they were as they said "Hola" to their new fans in various ports.

After six straight weeks on the road in this bus, it was going to be hard for any of the guys to look carefree. But for Duane it would have been impossible. The doctor had given him some prescription lozenges for his throat, but he looked too sick to party anywhere except in an isolation ward. He'd taken one look at his face in the mirror on the bus and decided he couldn't get on that yacht, not if he didn't want people to start asking why he looked so bad. No one was going to pay any attention to a note from his doctor. The press would have him dead and buried at sea before he knew what happened. Or, worse, just too old to be in the teenage market.

The truth was Duane felt bad, too. He ached all over. He didn't want to worry about sales figures and what the band should do next. He didn't even know what the band should do next. All he wanted to do was to go home and crawl into his bed and stay there for a month.

The problem was he didn't want to go home to his bed in Hollywood. His house there was all starkly modern with red adobe walls and black marble floors. He'd never felt that he belonged there. There wasn't even any food in the house.

No, when Duane had thought of home, there rose up in his mind the comforting picture of his old bedroom in his great-aunt's house in Dry Creek. He had come to that house kicking and screaming, but it had been the first home he'd ever really known. His mother, when she had been sober, had rented hotel rooms by the week.

When she wasn't sober, which was most of the time, they lived in her old car.

His great-aunt Cornelia had changed all that. Even though it had been only herself and Duane, she'd insisted on regular meals together, church on Sundays and hair that was combed for school. Even with his great-aunt gone, his old bedroom in that house drew Duane with its memories until he told everyone he was going to drive the tour bus up to Montana so he could spend some time in his old home.

He must have been delusional from the fever when he said that. He'd completely forgotten all of the reasons why it would be a very bad idea to go back to Dry Creek. The house in Dry Creek would be cold and empty. Great-Aunt Cornelia wouldn't be there to greet him with her stiff little smile. The cupboards wouldn't have any food, either. The people of Dry Creek still wouldn't know what to do with him.

And then there was Linda Morgan. Even a cold, empty house would still give him a warmer welcome than Linda would. She was the only woman who had ever rejected him—actually, she was the only woman who'd had the chance to reject him. But a man had to be a fool to go wandering into her territory when any number of other women would be happy to marry him. Assuming, of course, that he had any time to get to know them, which he unfortunately didn't.

No one had told him that being a rock star would ruin any life he'd planned to have. Although, the thought had been coming to him lately, that maybe he didn't really want a life after all. That maybe the idea of having a real life scared him to death. That when he asked Linda to marry him someday, he'd never really expected some-day to come. A man like him had no business getting married anyway. He'd never even seen a marriage up close. He wouldn't even know how to fake being a good husband.

All of which made him wonder why he was back here in Dry Creek.

"Yeah, it was the fever," Duane muttered to himself, which only set Phil off again.

Phil had refused to let Duane go off alone when he was sick and Duane didn't have the energy to fight him on it. Phil had his career invested in Duane's voice and Duane respected that. The rest of the band had started muttering about needing a new manager, but Duane held fast to Phil. The man had been with the band longer than the people who were now in the band. Phil had been the one constant when old band members left and new ones came in. He'd helped build their sales with his crazy promotional schemes; he deserved to be there more than any of the current band members. It was only fair.

"Forget about maybe having a medical clinic to preserve people's lives," Phil muttered quietly. "There's nothing else in this place, either. It's spooky. I thought when you said you were going home, there'd at least be—things."

Duane took a moment to swallow. If he went slowly, he could manage a sentence. "I told you Dry Creek was small."

Duane reminded himself that his decision to keep Phil was a good one. Although he might mention to the man that sometimes he talked a little too much. That conversation would have to wait until a time when Duane could also talk.

"Small is Boise. Or, at worst, Butte," Phil continued. "I didn't think a place could be *this* small and still be a town. There isn't even a Starbucks here."

"Coffee at café," Duane rasped. Maybe he could write out a note to Phil about the talking thing. Yes, that's what he'd do—when he had a pencil. And a piece of paper. And the heart to do it.

Phil peered out into the blackness. "I don't see any café. What's the name of the place? There should be a big neon sign on top of it."

"No name."

"Everything has a name." Phil turned to Duane in astonishment. "How do they get any business if they don't even have a name?"

Duane almost didn't speak, but he had to defend the café. "Business good."

He knew that for a fact because his old Sunday school teacher, Mrs. Hargrove, wrote him letters now and then and told him what was happening in Dry Creek. He had asked her to keep him informed about his great-aunt's house and Boots, but the letters tended to ramble until they included the whole town. The older woman was sensitive enough not to write about Linda, but she always said how the café was doing. Apparently, the café served a homemade blackberry pie these days that rivaled the pies his great-aunt used to bake. He'd been homesick ever since he heard that, remembering his great-aunt and the blackberry pies she used to serve.

Maybe all he'd come back here for was a piece of pie.

Phil was leaning closer to the tinted windows on the

right side of the bus. "I can't see anything else, either. And there's only one streetlight. How does anyone see anything in this place?"

Duane followed the direction of Phil's eyes. "One light's…enough."

Duane didn't have enough voice to explain that the residents of Dry Creek wanted to see the stars at night and too many streetlights would interfere with that. His great-aunt had carefully explained it to him. The town actually voted not to have the county put in more lights. He'd thought, at the time, that the town was voting itself back to the Dark Ages. In contrast, the Chicago he remembered had been lit up like a torch. He couldn't believe the people in Dry Creek weren't worried about crime.

Phil shook his head. "I've never seen this kind of darkness. And emptiness. What do people do with all this space? They should build a couple of skyscrapers. Or at least those big storage places. Even if people didn't want to be here, they could ship their stuff up and store it here. I wonder if they know how much money they could make with storage. Maybe then they could afford to put up some streetlights."

Duane cleared his throat so he could defend his town. "Good place." Duane swallowed. It had taken him years to make his peace with his feelings about the town, but he had. "They have stars—and national park for Custer's Last Stand."

"And they have *you,*" Phil said with a touch of enthusiasm as he turned to look fully at Duane. "I don't know why I didn't think of it earlier. You grew up in Dry Creek. People always love it when their celebrities have humble roots. The one thing I'll say for this place is that its roots couldn't be more humble if someone planned it that way."

Duane tried to speak, but nothing came out. He wasn't sure the people of Dry Creek would want to claim him the way they did General Custer even though the good general had lost his battle and Duane hadn't lost any of his fights in Dry Creek. Well, except maybe for the last one when he'd refused to meet Lance behind the old barn at his great-aunt's place the day he was leaving for the last time. Even General Custer insisted on knowing why he was going to battle and Lance had refused to talk about what was wrong, so Duane refused to fight him. The people of Dry Creek all probably thought he was a coward by now.

Phil continued thoughtfully. "That's right. Small-town boy makes good. People love that kind of stuff. We might even be able to tie it in to the Custer thing. You don't have any Native American blood in you, do you? This might even be better than the yacht. We can do a press conference right here in Dry Creek, childhood home of music legend Duane Enger. People would love it."

Duane shook his head. "My voice—"

Phil wasn't listening. He had a faraway look on his face. "I knew if I just kept thinking, something would come to me. It's been a while since I've had a brainstorm like this one. But I'm back in the game."

Phil turned to look at Duane and grinned. "We can do this. This could be our turnaround press conference. It could put us right back on top."

"But—"

Duane wasn't sure what the people of Dry Creek would think if he tried to use their town to promote himself. Everyone had been polite to him while he lived here, but it still wasn't the same as being one of them. On the streets of Chicago, he'd had no problem being himself. Of course, in Chicago no one cared who he was anyway, so it was easy. In Dry Creek, people hugged each other and had expectations of closeness. And niceness. And all of those things that made Duane nervous. He didn't know how he would have adjusted at all if he hadn't brought that guitar with him to hide behind.

"Don't thank me," Phil said. "It's the least I can do for you. I know you stood up for me with the rest of the band. But, don't worry. I won't let you down."

Duane opened his mouth and nothing came out. It might not be his vocal cords this time, though. He hadn't known Phil had found out about the secret meeting the band had held.

"Who told?"

Phil wasn't paying any attention. "Don't worry. You'll be better in no time. We'll keep the hot fluids coming. It will take a day or two to arrange things anyway. I'll need to think of an angle to give to the reporters. They're not all in Puerto Vallarta covering the rest of the band. But we still need an angle. It's not enough that you came home. You need a reason."

"I'm sick."

Phil frowned. "That won't be enough. You're not dying. I'd try the adoption angle, but everyone's done that one to death. I want something fresh. Besides, then you'd really need to adopt a baby and that would be complicated with the bus and all. And, since every-body's doing it, we'd have to get an unusual baby to make the news anyway."

"No," Duane squeaked in alarm as he slowed the bus down. He realized he was stopped in the middle of Dry Creek, but there wasn't any traffic so it didn't matter. Surely no one would let him adopt a baby; he'd never even been close to a new baby. He turned around so he could face Phil. He could only mouth the word. "No."

"That's what I'm saying. No dying. No baby." Phil tapped on his knee with his fingers as he thought. "I've got it. We'll say you're here to visit your old high school sweetheart. Don't I remember you wrote that one song—"

"No!" Duane half stood up. He even managed more than a squawk.

"You don't need to get so testy about it," Phil said. "But we have to say something. Your fans will want to know why you're here and not with the rest of the band in Mexico, partying your heart out. We need something the fans can grab hold of and feel good about. If your great-aunt was still alive, we could say you came to visit her. Sweet little old lady and all."

"Cornelia?"

Great-Aunt Cornelia had been a drill sergeant. That was the only thing that had saved them. He never could have stayed if she'd been sweet. He would have had to hitchhike back to Chicago. Great-Aunt Cornelia knew just how much softness he could handle and she never smothered him with sentimental stuff. He still missed her.

Phil didn't even stop. "But that's out. Visiting her

grave is too morbid. And, we certainly can't say you're here to go hunting for wild game or anything because that's a big no-no with some groups. And there's no water around for fishing. There's really no reason for you to be in Dry Creek."

Duane's head hurt. For years he would have agreed with Phil; there really was no reason for him to be in Dry Creek. But lately he'd started to miss the place although he couldn't quite say why. He looked out the bus window at the buildings just in case someone had added an opera house or something since he'd been here last. Of course, no one had. There were still only the usual places. The hardware store, the houses, the church— Duane stopped. "Say I came to visit the church."

Duane had gone to church when he lived with his great-aunt. It had been one of her rules. He hadn't paid much attention while he was in church, but he'd learned enough to know that churches were supposed to help people who were in need and he was definitely in need. Besides, he'd much rather go to a church service than have to explain to Linda why the papers all said he had come back to visit her. At least God wasn't likely to spit in his eye the way Linda would. He hoped not anyway. After all, Great-Aunt Cornelia had always said God was good at forgiving people.

Phil was nodding. "Church might work. It's a nice sentimental touch. It goes with the humble roots. And it would work in the Latin market."

Duane nodded as he turned around and switched on the ignition again. He was glad that was settled.

The band hovered on the precipice and Duane

wanted to do what he could to help. The band had already fallen apart once several years ago and reorganized with different people. He'd been the new one in the old band and now he was the oldest in the new band. And he felt it.

He missed the old band members; the ones who'd left so they could have normal lives.

The new members were trying louder and more aggressive sounds in their songs and Duane couldn't seem to get his voice right to make it happen. That's probably why his voice was strained. Sometimes the sheer noise of the new songs they played made him want to cover his ears. What if the others sensed that in him? In the old band, he had always been the one who was out there, ready to take the next step forward. Now, he was the one who was holding everything back.

Maybe that's why he was drawn to Dry Creek. He'd known what he wanted from his music when he was here.

"We'll say it's a pilgrimage thing," Phil said. "People like that kind of thing. A spiritual quest in the church of your childhood. This might work."

Duane passed the last house in Dry Creek and then saw the driveway to his great-aunt's house. There were no lights in the house, of course, because no one was living there now. Still, Duane felt satisfaction when he drove past the bent stop sign and turned the bus onto the driveway. He was back on Enger land at last. His grandfather had farmed this land. Coming to this place had made him feel, for the first time as a boy, that he wasn't just drifting through life. Granted, at the moment, it was muddy Enger land, but Duane's roots were here even if they were buried deep.

The bus was about halfway down the driveway when Duane felt the tires start to spin. He pressed on the gas and the tires spun some more. After the third time on the gas pedal, he was well and truly stuck in the mud. He didn't think Phil even realized what had gone wrong and Duane didn't have the voice to explain it all to him so he just said it was time to rest.

Phil was so involved in making notes in his planner that he didn't pay any attention to where they were anyway. Which was fine with Duane. He turned the ignition off and stretched a minute. Then he stood up and took one of the blankets draped over one of the seats and walked toward the bed area they had in the back of the bus. He was going to get some sleep. If Phil wanted to stay up all night and plan the church visit, that was fine. Let the man have his fun.

Duane lay down in the back of the bus and wrapped the blanket around him. Sleep never sounded so good.

Ten hours later, Duane heard a horn honking. He turned over and squinted at the soft light coming in the windows of the bus. It wasn't even full day yet. And his throat was on fire. So, he pulled the blanket over his head to block the emerging sun and hoped that Phil would go talk to whoever was outside. Phil was good at reasoning with people who were annoyed and that honking sounded as if someone was upset about something.

Linda stared at the big bus stuck in the middle of the Enger driveway. There were enough tinted windows in the thing to make it look like a caricature of a Mafia car. Only twenty times as big, of course. She wondered if a gamblers' tour to Las Vegas had gotten blown off course in the storm last night. There was no sane reason she could think of for a bus like this to be parked in a Dry Creek driveway. So much mud was spattered along the side of the bus that she couldn't read the name of the tour company. Sometimes tour buses came through here on the way to the park where Custer's Last Stand happened and this could be one of them.

Of course, there would be dozens of people milling around outside if that were the case. Once in a while, a tour bus would stop at the café and she knew tourists were never quiet. No, it couldn't be a tour bus.

Maybe Lucy was right about everything needing a name, after all. There was something unsettling about seeing things and not knowing their name. She didn't have a clue about where the bus came from or what it was or why it was here. That's why she'd pulled off the road and come in to check it out. Maybe Duane had decided to repair the old homestead and had sent a bus up filled with supplies. No, that didn't make any sense, either.

Linda's heart sank. Maybe Duane had sold the place. He certainly hadn't advertised for a buyer around this part of the country so that meant the new owners were probably from Hollywood. They'd probably tear the old house down and build some ugly mansion. Boots would be totally lost if they did that. He still walked over to the old house every day just to smell the familiar things. Not that Duane had probably bothered to find that out.

It was just like Duane to sell the house without checking with anyone in Dry Creek. But that must be what happened. This bus surely made it look that way. That bus was even big enough to serve as temporary lodging for workmen while the mansion was being built.

There was one of the workers now. Linda saw a man open the door of the bus and step down. He didn't look very strong, but she supposed Hollywood builders might have enough sophisticated tools that they didn't need to be strong to do their jobs.

"Can I help you?" the man said as he closed the door to the bus and stepped closer to her. "We're not blocking anything, are we?"

"No, not a problem," Linda said as she tried to give the man a cheerful smile. "Sorry if I woke you up. I suppose you're with the new owners?"

The man blinked at her. "Maybe."

"Oh." Linda swallowed. That was a clear "none of your business" answer. "Well, if there's anything I can do to help you, let me know. And welcome to Dry Creek."

"I could use some help finding the church."

"Oh, well, that's easy." Linda turned to point. "It's the white building on the other side of town. You see the cross?"

The man nodded.

"You can usually find Pastor Curtis at the hardware store during the mornings. He works there some. If you need to talk to him, that is."

"Oh, we'll need to talk to him," the man said. "The Jazz Man is on a pilgrimage."

"Jazz—you mean?" Linda looked frantically at the

bus. She wished she could see in those tinted windows. Or wipe the mud off the side of the bus and read what it said.

The man nodded proudly. "He's going to meet God, right here in Dry Creek, his childhood home."

"He's here?" Linda asked. She took a step forward involuntarily and then took two steps back. "Here himself."

She wondered if there was another Jazz Man who had grown up around here.

The man continued to beam and nod. "Isn't it great?"

Linda swallowed. *Great* wasn't the word she would use to describe it. *Astonishing,* maybe. But *great,* no.

"We'll have to start making arrangements, of course. Are there any hotels around? We'll need to reserve some rooms."

"Mrs. Hargrove has a room she rents out sometimes. It's over her garage."

The man frowned, but he took out a notebook from his pocket and opened it up. "I suppose it will have to do. What is the name of her place?"

"Name?" Linda was finally one hundred percent convinced that Lucy was right and that every business needed a name. "I don't think it has one yet."

"Oh."

"But you can find it easy enough. It's just down the street from my café."

"You own the café? Are you serving breakfast yet?"

Linda nodded. "As soon as I get there and open up."

"I'll be there. I don't suppose you have soup on the menu?"

She shrugged. "I could heat some up for you. It's leftover from yesterday, though. Vegetable beef."

"Perfect. I'll stop in before I go over to the church. Or should I go to the church first? That sounds more pious, doesn't it?"

"I don't know."

"Oh, well, it doesn't matter. The reporters aren't here yet. Besides, it's Duane Enger who's found religion. Not me."

Linda was speechless. What was the man talking about? She didn't mean to be skeptical about another person's faith, but the Duane she knew hadn't spared a thought for God. Duane had gone to church to please his great-aunt and that was all. "You're talking about the real God? Not some strange guru cult thing?"

The man drew himself up to his full height. "Of course I'm talking about the real God."

"Oh, well then—" Linda stammered. She could have asked the man if he used real butter and gotten the same reaction. "Congratulations."

The man nodded. "I think we'll have Duane sing a solo for church to celebrate his return to the faith. That should make for some good pictures. You have choir robes, don't you?"

Linda nodded her head. That settled it for her. The Duane she knew would never wear a choir robe. "Sort of. But they're old. And faded. They've been packed away for a couple of years. No one usually wears them for a solo anyway."

"What color are they? I hope they're not a metallic gray. That doesn't show up so well in pictures."

"They're blue with white collars."

"Good." The man nodded. "Blue is good for pictures. And it looks so religious, if you know what I mean. You always see it in the old religious paintings. Why do you suppose that is?"

"You really should be talking to Pastor Curtis about this. I think those robes would need to be cleaned if anyone was going to wear one."

"I'll do that. Right after breakfast."

There didn't seem to be anything else to say so Linda nodded. Maybe the man was crazy. She'd been looking at those tinted windows for five minutes now and she didn't see any movement inside the bus. Maybe the man was some kind of stalker who went to the childhood homes of celebrities and told everyone the celebrity was inside a bus when it was really empty. It would be kind of creepy, but—

Suddenly, Linda realized she and this man were the only ones standing here in the middle of the Engers' driveway. "I should get to the café."

The man smiled. "I'll be there for breakfast in a few minutes."

Linda turned. "You might want to stop at the hardware store first."

She started walking back to her car.

There were always lots of men sitting around the old woodstove in the hardware store early in the morning before the café opened. Charley Nelson and Elmer Maynard particularly made that a habit now that they'd retired from ranching. They sat there and waited for the café to open. Both of them had lived enough years on this earth to be able to spot a crazy person if they talked to him for more than a minute. She'd stop and warn them to be on guard.

And, just to be on the safe side, she'd bring out her heavy metal spatula from the kitchen when she served this man his breakfast. She could slip it into the pocket of her big apron; it wouldn't look as much out of place as the butcher knife would. Besides, the man didn't look tall enough to overpower her, so the spatula should keep her safe and secure enough. A solid rap with that should discourage him.

In a way, she told herself as she got in her car and drove the rest of the way to her café, she hoped the man *was* crazy. That meant Duane Enger wasn't anywhere near Dry Creek. Even a spatula wouldn't do much to protect her from Duane.

She'd opened the café door before she remembered she had something even stronger than a kitchen utensil to rely on here. She had the power of prayer. She was still new in her faith and she had to confess she was too used to solving her own problems. She needed to learn to ask God for help more; Mrs. Hargrove and Pastor Curtis had both told her that.

"He wants you to turn to Him, dear," Mrs. Hargrove was forever saying. "You're His child now. He cares about you."

So, after Linda went into the kitchen part of the café to start the coffee, she took her Bible out of her purse and started to read the Psalms. The words did make her feel better.

After all, if God could keep someone safe in the valley of the shadow of death, He could protect her from a man having delusions of grandeur in a mud puddle in the Enger driveway. She'd still carry the spatula for backup insurance, though. The Bible talked about wise and prudent women, too. There was no point in being foolish and going off unprepared for problems.

Chapter Three

Duane woke up several hours later and squinted. Enough light was coming in the tinted windows to let him know it was midmorning. He wished it was still dark. His eyelids felt as though they were coated with sandpaper. Fortunately, the fire in his throat was gone and he could swallow without pain. He tried to say his name and an encouragingly full voice came out briefly before turning to a squeak. If he had some coffee, he might actually be able to talk normally.

Something had pulled Duane out of his sleep and he couldn't figure out what it was. Phil was obviously not in the bus. The rain must have stopped, because Duane couldn't hear it. No one was around. He knew the bus was stuck in the mud at his great-aunt's place. It couldn't have been the sound of another vehicle coming up to the bus that had awakened him. Nothing but a tow truck could get in and there were no tow trucks in Dry Creek. If anyone was here, they had walked down the driveway.

Then he heard it. A quick, decisive knock on the door of the bus.

Phil wouldn't ordinarily knock, but maybe he had his hands full with something and couldn't pull the door open. The thought encouraged Duane since that probably meant his manager was on the other side of the door holding several cups of coffee.

Duane ran his hand through his hair as he walked down the aisle of the bus toward the door. He'd have to find Mrs. Hargrove and ask about getting the key to his great-aunt's place. Well, it was technically his place now, although he never thought of it that way.

Great-Aunt Cornelia would be the first one to tell him to get his hair combed before he went out and he had a stubborn spot that resisted his finger combing. If he could get inside the house, he could take a shower. The water would be cold, but it would be better than nothing. It should, at least, tame his hair. Maybe he'd be able to turn the utilities on without too much trouble.

Duane stepped down toward the bus door and pushed it open.

"Oh."

Duane grunted and took another swipe at his hair. The sun was bright outside and it hurt his eyes. He blinked anyway. What was *she* doing here? He always thought that when he saw her again, he would be looking good. Like maybe coming off a heart-pounding concert where there were screaming fans on the side-lines and reporters taking pictures.

Instead, he suddenly remembered the ketchup stain on his T-shirt from the hamburger he'd eaten outside of Salt Lake yesterday. A T-shirt he'd just slept in. And he hadn't shaved since he left San Pedro. Or even brushed his teeth last night. There wasn't a fan in sight. And his hair looked wild.

"You're really here," Linda said to him as she narrowed her eyes and examined him suspiciously.

Duane winced. She would have given a warmer welcome to a spider crawling up her arm. And she hated spiders.

"My bus," Duane croaked out. His voice was not as strong as he had hoped or he would remind her it was also his land. The people in this part of the world might not be impressed by rock stars, but they were big on the rights of someone who owned land to be on that land, even if they were stuck in the mud and looked as if they'd slept on a park bench during a hurricane.

Right now, Duane couldn't speak all of the words he'd need to explain that he didn't usually look like this. That he was successful and had money in the bank. In two banks, in fact. He even had gel that would tame his hair if he just had a chance to get to it.

Linda held out a brown bag. "Your friend, Phil, asked me to bring this out to you."

He saw the forced smile Linda gave him. Her face was thinner than he remembered and her hair was definitely more subdued. She'd let it go back to her natural brown color and it looked good, all sleek and shapely. She was wearing jeans and an oversize chef's apron that covered a white T-shirt. Of course, there were no ketchup stains on her T-shirt. No hair problems, either. She could have stepped off the cover of a gourmet food magazine.

Duane needed coffee. There were two containers in

the bag and as long as one of them was coffee he was okay. He'd drink almost anything if it'd give him his voice back so he could talk to Linda. "Thanks."

Linda stiffened. "No need to thank me. There's some hot soup there, too."

Duane reached out and took the bag while he had the chance. "How much?"

"It's already been paid for."

"Oh." Duane looked at the clutter tray he kept near the driver's seat. He pulled out a twenty-dollar bill that was curled up there between several singles.

He offered the twenty to Linda. "Tip."

Linda's eyes snapped as if he'd insulted her. "You don't need to give me that kind of money."

Okay, so Linda was finally talking to him.

Duane's head hurt. Giving someone a generous tip was supposed to be a good thing and, when he got his voice back, he intended to tell Linda that. He would try to tell her now, but the sun was shining down on her and he just wanted to take another minute to look at her.

"Your hair—" Duane said. The sun was turning strands of her brown hair into gold. It was beautiful. She should have let it go natural years ago.

Linda flushed. "I know it's nothing like it used to be. I don't take time to streak it anymore. I have to get Lucy off to school before I get to the café and—well, you don't want to know all about that. You probably don't have to worry about getting anyone anywhere, not even a dog."

"But—"

"Sorry, it's none of my business who you live with, dog or otherwise," Linda interrupted, looking determined to be polite. "So, Phil tells me you've come back here to sing a big, dramatic solo in our church."

"What?" The word started with a squeak and ended with a whisper.

"I hope it's not supposed to be a secret. He's back at the café now using my phone to make some calls. Cell phone reception isn't very good here. People don't usually have a press conference after singing in church, but I'm sure you know what you're doing. After all, it's your show."

Duane shook his head. His voice might be gone, but he didn't want Linda to believe what Phil said about him giving a show. The agreement last night was that Duane would visit the church—*visit* the church—as in going to a church service and putting a big donation in the offering plate. He hadn't agreed to call the kind of attention to himself Linda was talking about. Duane knew that people around here took their church seriously. He didn't want to come in looking like some big shot throwing his weight around and demanding to do a solo in front of reporters.

He'd been nearly invisible when he'd been here as a teenager; the cowboys, like his friend Lance, had overshadowed everyone else. Duane hadn't expected any big attention from the church back then and he certainly didn't expect it now. He'd played guitar for people in the café and that was it. He'd always wanted to keep a low profile in Dry Creek anyway. He wasn't really accepted here and he knew it. He saw no reason to remind everyone else of the fact. Besides, they all knew he hated church; that much had been obvious.

Linda moved slightly. "Well, I need to get back to the café."

The one person who had seemed to really accept him in Dry Creek had been Linda. She'd opened her heart to him when he'd been a lonely boy and never turned it away from him. He'd later thought she was like sunshine after a long Chicago winter.

And then he'd made the mistake of asking her to marry him. He never should have done that. He was in some dreamlike fog when he asked, but he should have known better. A man like him had no business thinking of having a wife or a family. Especially not a sweet wife like Linda. He'd grown up in a car, for pity's sake. A car that reeked of alcohol. His only friend back in Chicago had been a homeless man named Pete who had taught him to play jazz songs on the guitar. Duane figured he had nothing to offer a family.

Still, seeing Linda here today in the sunshine made him long for a future with her anyway, even if he couldn't have it.

"Don't go," Duane tried to say, but he couldn't make any sound and Linda just turned to walk away.

Duane looked down at the coffee he held in his hands. He hoped it gave him his voice back because he needed to speak to Phil. And then he needed to talk to Linda.

Linda looked back at the bus when she reached the main road. She'd walked over to the bus instead of driving and she was glad she had. It gave her a few minutes to pull herself together before she got back to the café.

She stood a moment at the bent-heart stop sign that marked the gravel road crossing by the Enger driveway. There were several plastic red flowers planted in the dirt at the bottom of that sign as a reminder of the love of the eloping couple from twenty-six years ago.

Linda had to blink to stop from crying. One miracle in the love department was probably all that would happen in Dry Creek for a while. Besides, she couldn't stand here all day. Even if Doris June Hargrove and Curtis Nelson had their happily-ever-after, that didn't mean God was going to give one to her and Duane. Linda didn't even have the hope needed to pray for one.

The day was still overcast and the ground was damp as she kept walking back to the café. Everything smelled musty, like wet earth. She hadn't worn a jacket and she crossed her arms to warm herself. The day had turned chilly. Or maybe it was just her. There had been nothing in the day when she got up to warn her that her worst nightmare was coming true.

Apparently Phil wasn't crazy after all. Duane was back there in his black tour bus, looking very much like the rock star he was. She wished she had believed he was really in the bus, because then she would have used the walk over here to think of something clever to say to him.

Instead, she'd sounded like what she was—a delivery person from the local café. And, a bit of a shrew. She couldn't believe she'd practically asked if he was living with someone. His private life was certainly none of her business. Technically, it wasn't even any of her concern if he had gotten a dog to replace Boots.

Thinking of Boots reminded her that she'd have to

give Mrs. Hargrove a call and warn her that Duane was back in town. She hoped Boots wouldn't be as shocked to see Duane as she had been. Then she'd have to call Lucy. It was Saturday and her sister was at home, but she'd never forgive Linda if she missed a chance to see the Jazz Man up close and in person.

She wondered how long Duane would be here.

Linda shook her head. She had always thought that, if she saw Duane again, she would say something to make him regret leaving Dry Creek. Make him regret leaving her. She certainly didn't think she'd be taking a righteous stand about some mammoth tip he wanted to give her. Now that she had a moment to think about it, she decided her reaction had made her sound as if she had needed the twenty dollars and had been too embarrassed to accept it.

Linda knew God didn't care more about some people than others because they had larger bank accounts. And, truthfully, she was happy with the money she made in her café, especially now that they'd started setting the pie money aside for Lucy's college fund so that worry was covered.

It's just that Linda didn't like the feeling that Duane might look at her and be glad he wasn't married to her. Of course, if he did it probably would have nothing to do with money. Cold hard cash was only the beginning of the differences in their lives now. Duane was probably relieved not to be with her because she'd grown old and boring while he'd turned into a glamorous rock star without a care in the world. He probably knew without asking that she didn't own one designer pair of jeans, but had three old fuzzy bathrobes instead.

Linda had known since her visit to Hollywood that she wouldn't fit in with Duane's road trip life, but she hadn't known until this morning that she'd turned into the same kind of disapproving adult she and Duane had complained about all those years ago. She probably would never have to admit it to him, but she didn't even like the rock music he played anymore. It was too loud and it made her want to turn the volume down.

She shook her head. She had indeed turned into her mother. It wasn't a happy thought.

There were several people on the porch of the café when Linda walked up and she doubted it was because she was serving Irish oatmeal for breakfast this week.

"Is Duane Enger really back?" Charley asked.

The whole group of men from the hardware store had come over as they usually did. Now that they were retired, they all had too much time on their hands. Charley stood a little apart from the others. He leaned against one of the posts at the end of the café porch with a wool cap on his head and a denim coat on his back.

Linda nodded as she put her hand on the knob to the door and then looked over her shoulder at the other men standing near her. "He's back there in that bus stuck in his great-aunt's drive."

"I always told Cornelia that she needed more gravel on that road of hers," Charley muttered. "Every time it drizzles, the whole stretch of it puddles up. I was going to bring in a load of rocks from my ranch for her. But then, of course, there was no need—"

"No one cares about the gravel. What's the man here for?" Elmer asked with a frown and a worried look at Linda. Elmer's white hair might be thinning, but he looked ready to do battle. "I never thought that one would be back. Especially since his great-aunt isn't here no more."

"Neither did I." Linda gave a smile of thanks to everyone. She could always count on the people in Dry Creek to stick up for her.

"I thought you were sweet on Lance now anyway," Elmer added. "I kind of like him. He says he's going to play horseshoes with me some Sunday afternoon. Not many folks play horseshoes anymore."

Charley nodded. "I was voting for Lance, too. Especially since he joined the church. That Enger fella never did like going to church. You could tell. He sat there and frowned at the floor."

"I'm not the reason Duane's back here." Linda opened the door. She'd get that settled with people up front. She didn't want any rumors floating around.

"Not the reason?" Charley asked indignantly as he followed her into the café. "You jolly well better be the reason. I don't care who he thinks he is, you always were too good for him. He sure better be back here to see you. He owes you. He got his start right here in your café."

"It was our café, remember? He was my partner."

"That means he owes you even more."

"No, it's okay," Linda said as she walked to the kitchen with the men following.

"We'll see what Lance says about that," Elmer said.

Linda turned slightly just before she walked through the doorway to the kitchen. It was nice to know some people stood by her. "Coffee, everyone? It's on the house."

* * *

Duane cut his face while shaving. He couldn't find his electric shaver and he was lucky to find one of those disposable plastic ones. He'd used up the last of the water in the portable tank the bus held just so he could scrape the whiskers off his face and brush his teeth. And all so that he would look respectable when he walked into Dry Creek.

He'd been on stage at the Greek Theatre in Hollywood and hadn't been this nervous about his looks.

Of course, now he had cuts all over his clean-shaven chin. He looked as though he'd just been attacked by wild birds. Fortunately he'd had enough water to slick down his hair and wipe his face so he appeared to have at least survived the attack with some dignity.

There weren't any more houses around in the day than there had been last night. Duane figured Phil was somewhere trying to get people to build something tall. Of course, the people of Dry Creek would not listen.

In his years on the road, Duane had come to appreciate the fact that Dry Creek never changed. He could read Mrs. Hargrove's letters and picture everything. Even now, as he walked through town, he could look at each house and know who lived in it. He hadn't met the family that moved into old man Gossett's house yet, but he'd heard about the woman and her kids. Mrs. Hargrove always wrote about any new people and the weddings. Dry Creek had a rash of weddings in the last couple of years that had delighted the older woman and, frankly, astonished him. People didn't seem to hesitate to get married in this town. Maybe they didn't know the divorce statistics.

Still, it was amazing that he knew so many people here. If he walked down his street in Hollywood, he wouldn't know even one neighbor. And he certainly wouldn't know if they were happily married or had children or aches and pains or any of the things Mrs. Hargrove seemed to know about her neighbors.

Duane had forgotten how it felt to *know* people. Not that he'd known that many in his life. When the band was on tour, they never stayed anyplace long enough to know anyone except each other. There was no time for girlfriends or games of neighborhood basketball. When it got right down to it, Phil was the closest friend he had, now that he was pretty sure Lance had crossed him off his list. He'd sent a couple of postcards to Lance at first, but had never gotten any response.

Duane took another look around as he walked by the hardware store and then he stopped. The door was opening and someone was coming out.

"Duane!" the man called.

Duane squinted through his sunglasses and recognized Pastor Curtis.

Duane hoped the pastor would realize that the reason Duane was wearing sunglasses was because his eyes hurt and not because he was so vain that he expected anyone to recognize him in Dry Creek. Well, of course, people would *recognize* him, but not because he was a celebrity. They'd know him because they'd known him since he first got here and his great-aunt Cornelia had made him stand up in church when they asked if there was anyone new in the service.

"I hear you want to sing a big solo for us," the pastor said. The man's smile was steady and firm. "I think your manager, Phil, said it would be like something we've never seen before, something spectacular."

Duane shook his head. "No spectacle— Not worthy—"

The pastor nodded. "None of us are really worthy to praise God in song—or any other way, for that matter, so don't let that hold you back."

"No, I—" Duane started again.

"We'll talk about it when you come to my office. Your manager said one o'clock this afternoon would work. We'll work out the details then."

Duane nodded. If he could keep drinking coffee, maybe his voice would be fully recovered by this afternoon. And he might even think of what to say to the pastor by then. Maybe singing a solo for the church would be okay even if it was for the publicity. The pastor sure didn't seem worried about anything.

Besides, it was obvious if anyone looked at the preliminary sales of their recent CD, that they needed some kind of help. Maybe the band did need to change their sound. Duane was the lead singer and the lead guitarist so, if the band needed to change, he had to be a part of it. Maybe they did need to be louder and more aggressive in their sounds. If he sang in church, maybe God would give him a little help in return. It wouldn't need to be much. Just enough to get him going in the new direction. When the band got back together in Hollywood in a couple of weeks, they'd start working on some new songs. That would settle everyone down. Things would be good again.

By now Duane had reached the café. He heard Linda's voice even before he stepped on the porch. He wondered if she even remembered that his dream had been for them both to go to Hollywood and become music stars.

He supposed it was all for the best that she hadn't wanted to stay with him when she came for that visit. Not all that much had changed in the eight years that he'd been gone. His career was, once again, hanging by a thread. Things had seemed to go backward instead of forward for him. He wasn't still living in a car as he had been in Chicago, but the bus wasn't that much bigger and it still was never parked in one place for long. He might have lots of money in the bank, but he didn't have a real life. He wouldn't want Linda to be living like that with him. She had a nice secure future here in Dry Creek. She had her own business, one she'd built herself. No one would call her up one day and say her sales had hit rock bottom and her time in the spotlight was over. Things were steady for her. She had a home; she had a family.

He wouldn't want to take any of that away from her, not when he could honestly say he envied her.

Chapter Four

Linda was hiding in the kitchen. Oh, she had a couple of pancakes on the grill and a few biscuits in the oven, but she was really hiding instead of cooking. Not that her customers cared. They were sitting out in the main part of the café looking like warriors, ready to defend her from any slight or hurt that might come her way.

Linda always thought that one reason she and Lucy had managed so well without either of their parents was because they had so many volunteer parents in Dry Creek. Those older men out front had not been shy about standing in as grandfathers to them.

Right now, they were keeping an eye on Phil. The man was on the pay phone at the far counter of the café, but he kept his voice low and didn't seem to be bothering anyone too much. Still, the grandfathers probably wanted to be sure he wasn't causing trouble, especially since she'd asked them much earlier if they thought he was normal in the head.

Linda heard the outside door to the café open and she tensed up. She knew it had to be Duane walking in.

She'd known since she handed him his soup and coffee that he'd be showing up at the café. For one thing, according to Phil, there was no coffeemaker in the tour bus. That meant they'd need to get their coffee from the café. The Duane she knew would always drink more than one cup of the stuff.

Linda felt like sitting down and having a cup of coffee herself. Or maybe some of that herbal tea that was supposed to be good for stress. Even some plain hot water might steady her nerves.

God must be testing her, Linda thought as she flipped the pancakes. She supposed she should be grateful it was Duane that He had sent instead of a plague of locusts. At least she knew Duane would be easy to get rid of. He wasn't even interested in Dry Creek. He was only here for a publicity stunt. Linda had put together that much from what she'd overheard of Phil's telephone conversations. The two men would be gone as soon as Duane sang his song in the church and had his press conference. She was sure of that.

All Duane's coming to Dry Creek meant to her was a little more business for her café.

Linda scooped the pancakes off the grill and put them on two of her new white dinner plates. Business was already so good she'd ordered a whole new inventory of dishes after Christmas. Maybe if she made enough extra from the reporters who were coming she'd go ahead and order that jukebox. She almost had enough saved anyway. Some bacon was warming at the side of the grill and Linda put that next to the pancakes. There was already butter and syrup on the tables, so she lifted the two plates and headed for the doorway.

She couldn't afford to hide away all morning. She had a business to run.

Linda stepped out into the main part of the café and blinked. Duane was there all right.

Somehow though he didn't look as heartbreaking-handsome as she had expected. He was wearing dark sunglasses so she couldn't see his blue eyes, which was a blessing since they'd always been her downfall. His hair was damp so it looked more brown than usual and it was lanky as if he'd washed it, but hadn't used shampoo. And his face had a whole bunch of little cuts on it.

"What happened to you?" Linda asked.

There was total silence in the café. No one lifted a coffee cup or shuffled a foot.

Duane took a deep breath and looked at Linda.

"Razor." Duane answered her question. Then, because he didn't want her to be alarmed he added, "Shaving. And, I'm not contagious. Voice strained."

Duane congratulated himself. The coffee had worked. His words didn't sound like the scraping of a rusty hinge. He might look as though he'd had a rough night, but his voice was back.

There was more silence as Duane stood there and looked around. He hadn't realized Linda had completed the plans for the café that they'd talked about before he'd left Dry Creek. He wondered if she remembered that they had started the business together, partly to give themselves a place to perform and partly to make some money to get a start in life.

"You did it," Duane said. "Fifties linoleum on the floor."

"It's not real linoleum," Linda said as she walked farther into the main area and set a couple of plates of pancakes in front of the old men. "The fake stuff wears better."

"But it looks just right. You can almost see Duke Ellington playing the blues in a place like this. I bet the place really rocks."

Duane had finished the sentence before his voice began to strain.

Linda looked up from setting the plates on the table and faced Duane. "I don't have live music here so there's nothing to rock. Sometimes I play some classical stuff on the stereo, but that's it."

"You don't sing? I always pictured you singing here like we used to—I mean, without the guitar, of course, but—"

Linda frowned at him. "I don't have time to sing anymore."

"Oh, I'm sorry."

"Don't be," Linda said. "I just grew up. That's all."

Duane saw movement out of the corner of his eyes and noticed that the older men who had been sitting eating their breakfast had now all stood up and were looking at him.

"It's all right," Linda said as she smiled at the older men. "I think the biscuits are about done. I'll be right back out with them and some of that honey butter you all like."

Linda turned and walked to the kitchen.

The men went back to their chairs and sat down.

Duane couldn't help but notice that they all sat staring at him and not looking the least bit friendly.

"I didn't mean anything by it," Duane said as he walked over to the table. "How was I to know she doesn't sing anymore? She loves to sing."

Duane recognized all of the men. Charley Nelson. Elmer Maynard. Burt Jones. He'd known them when he was growing up around here. He knew they'd thought he was a punk kid in those days, with his guitar and his ragged hair. Back then he hadn't expected them to respect him and hadn't particularly cared if they did or not. But now he just might care a little. He saw how they looked after Linda and he was glad they did. He met Charley's eyes.

The older man finally spoke. "You would have known that she doesn't sing anymore if you ever called her up on the telephone."

"Lance calls her," Elmer offered. "And he stops by the café to see her in person. Which I'm sure she likes very much. Women do, you know."

Duane winced. He'd never thought about Lance and Linda together, but it made sense.

"She told me we didn't suit," Duane finally answered the older men because it seemed he had no choice. His voice was starting to feel even more strained, but he kept going on. "I didn't think she'd exactly welcome a call from me."

Duane could see none of the men knew that. They looked at each other as if for confirmation.

"When did she tell you a fool thing like that?" Charley finally looked back at Duane and asked.

"When she came to Hollywood that summer," he whispered. "After her mother died."

"Well." Charley frowned. "Did you do something to set her off?"

Duane shook his head and tried his best to give sound to his words. "I can't think of anything."

"Well," Charley said again and ran his hand through his hair. "I sure don't figure women."

The men were all silent for a minute.

Finally Charley shook his head. "I wonder if Mrs. Hargrove knew. That woman never tells me anything. Here all this time I thought Linda was nursing a broken heart and she's the one who got rid of you."

Duane winced. He supposed that was about the size of it.

Elmer cleared his throat quietly and nudged Charley with his elbow. "Keep your voice down. Linda won't like us talking about her business."

"Well, it's not only her business," Charley protested. "It's mine, too. I've worried myself sick over that girl. I don't know how many times Mrs. Hargrove and I have prayed that Linda would get over him." Charley jerked his head in the direction of Duane. "And now I find out she wasn't even interested in him anyway so there was nothing at all to get over."

"I think that's a bit strong," Duane said. His voice was going, but he could do a hearty whisper. "She had said she'd marry me once."

Duane knew he shouldn't have said that the minute the words left his mouth. It wasn't Linda's fault he wasn't marriage material. He certainly didn't fault her for refusing to be part of his delusion.

"Now, when was that?" Charley asked. "I didn't know that, either. How am I supposed to be an honorary grandfather to the girl when no one tells me anything?"

"Hey, you're not the only grandfather here," Elmer protested. "I look out for Linda and Lucy, too. Lance does, too, you know. Not as a grandfather, of course, but—"

"Long time ago." Duane's voice cracked and his whisper ended with a hoarse croak. He still remembered the day Lance had gotten so angry with him. Duane wished now that he'd taken the time to fight his friend one more time before he left. Maybe then he wouldn't be feeling the urge to do so now. It was one thing for him to realize he'd make a lousy husband; it was another thing for his best friend to move in on his girl when he was gone.

"Well, I hope Lucy isn't set to marry someone and no one told us," Charley muttered. Charley looked over at where Phil stood beside the only phone in the café. "Isn't he done yet? I need to call Mrs. Hargrove. Somebody needs to talk to these girls and find out what's what."

"No, no." Duane put up his hand. His voice was gone, but he kept trying to talk anyway. The men would have to read his lips for this one. "Not because of me."

Everyone got quiet when the door to the kitchen opened out again. Linda was walking back with a pot of coffee in one hand and a plate of biscuits in the other.

He didn't need Linda to hear about this conversation, Duane thought as he reached for one of the empty cups that stood beside an unused place setting. He patiently waited for Linda to fill the cups of all of the older men before he held his cup out hopefully.

Duane mouthed the word *please*.

Linda nodded and silently poured him a cup of coffee, as well.

Duane felt the hot liquid slide down his throat with his first gulp. Nothing had felt so good going down his throat since his earlier cup of coffee. Linda's café might not have fancy coffee concoctions, but it had a good, strong brew. Duane walked over to a table and sat down so he'd have a place to rest his cup.

He looked right across at the opposite wall when he lifted his cup again. Now, why hadn't he seen what was there earlier?

"My guitar," Duane said and pointed. It was that old Silvertone guitar he'd brought with him from Chicago. He hadn't even had an extra pair of socks, but he'd had that guitar.

"Well, you left it here." Linda put the empty pot of coffee down on the table and pulled an order pad from the pocket of her apron. She didn't seem too eager to take his order. "If you want it back, you're welcome to it."

Duane shook his head.

"Of course, you wouldn't want it back. What am I thinking? Nothing here is good enough for you any-more."

Duane shook his head a little more emphatically. "I just got a different guitar. That's all."

Linda frowned even more at that.

"Voice going," Duane said, just so she'd know his argument time was limited.

"I suppose, though…" Linda paused, looking even more disgruntled. "Now that I think of it, it's not just the guitar that belongs to you."

She swept her arm around to show the café. "I forgot we used your money to get started."

Duane shrugged his shoulders. "It's okay."

"No, no, I'll pay you back," Linda said as she started to walk to the kitchen. When she got to the kitchen door, she turned around to look at Duane. "What was it? Twelve hundred dollars, wasn't it?"

Duane nodded. He'd earned that money bucking bales at the Elkton Ranch the summer before he and Linda had started the café. He knew how much he'd made to the penny. He and Lance had worked side by side. Duane had never worked so hard in his life or been so proud of his paychecks. Lance had bought his first horse; Duane had given his money to Linda for the café.

"Did she say twelve hundred dollars?" Elmer turned to Duane and asked after Linda had walked back into the kitchen. "What's she doing with that kind of money around here?"

Duane frowned. That was too much money to keep in an old coffee can in the kitchen. Linda was practically inviting thieves to come help themselves. Still, it hadn't been his idea that she keep cash around here and, the way the old men were looking at him, they must think it had been.

Duane just shook his head and reached for his coffee cup again. He'd only taken a couple of more gulps before he heard the front door to the café open.

The girlish squeal coming from the door made Duane turn around in his chair. Oh, no. There were a half dozen young teenage girls pointing at him. He slumped down in the chair, hoping they were looking at someone else. He didn't look anything like his fan photo so maybe they wouldn't recognize him even if they thought he was here.

"I told you he'd be here," the blond girl in the middle announced proudly. "He used to play his guitar and sing here, you know. Right in the café here."

Duane tried to smile at the girls. He reminded himself he needed all of the fans he could get these days. He couldn't afford to forget that. Even if he didn't look like his picture.

The door to the kitchen swung open and Linda stepped out.

"Lucy!" Linda said as she walked toward the group of girls. "I said I'd come get you after I've served everyone breakfast. Don't tell me you drove here? You know your learner's permit only lets you drive with an adult in the car."

"Ben brought me," Lucy said with a grin. "He said he'll drive me whenever I want to go someplace."

"My grandson?" Charley half stood up. "Where is he anyway?"

"Trying to find a place to park that's out of the mud," Lucy said.

"That sounds like Ben," Charley said smugly as he sat down. He turned to the other older men at the table. "There's nothing impulsive about Ben. Very orderly, that boy. He's not going to go breaking some girl's heart."

Duane noticed Lucy wasn't listening to the older men. She was walking over to the guitar hanging on the wall.

Duane wasn't listening to the men, either. When he'd left Dry Creek, Lucy had been seven or eight years old. She'd been charming then, but she was beautiful now. It struck him, while he was looking at her, that he could have been her brother-in-law if things had gone as he'd dreamed with Linda. Surely, Lucy was too young to be riding around the countryside with some boy named Ben.

"I hope Ben has a driver's license," Duane said. His voice wasn't as powerful as he wanted so he added a scowl for effect.

Everyone stopped talking.

Finally, Lucy blinked at Duane. "He's sixteen. He has a license."

Duane found he was still worried about Lucy riding around the countryside with a boy who was sixteen. "Too young for a car."

"The boy doesn't really have a car," Charley said. "He borrows the work pickup from the ranch. The thing won't go over thirty miles an hour."

Slow pickups were just as bad in Duane's opinion, but he didn't have the voice to speak out all of his objections. He was even surprised he had objections. He was acting like Lucy *was* his little sister, but she wasn't. He didn't have any siblings. No relatives at all, at this point in the game. His mother had died of alcoholism shortly after he moved here to his great-aunt's place and his father had left the scene when Duane was born.

He'd done fine without parental interference; he didn't know why he wanted to make sure Lucy had some rules to guide her. Maybe because she looked so young with that excitement on her face. She reminded him of Linda at that age.

"I just wanted to show you where we put your letter," Lucy said. She was standing by his old guitar and Duane didn't know what she was talking about. Then he saw the letter, framed and hanging by his guitar.

Duane nodded and smiled. He recognized the graphics; she had one of his fan letters.

"Linda said you didn't write it yourself," Lucy said as she looked at her sister.

"Get too many," Duane muttered, as he studied the linoleum on the floor. It was common practice for people to send out canned fan letters. Everyone knew that. It was the way things were done. Still, it made him feel rotten when he saw the glow fade on Lucy's face.

"Should have written," Duane whispered. But it was too late. He looked up and Lucy was looking at him as if he'd just given away her prize kitten.

"But I wrote in my letter that I was from Dry Creek," she said. She'd taken the framed letter off the wall and was holding it to her. "I thought you'd read that one for sure. This is your *home.*"

Duane had told the staff years ago to separate Mrs. Hargrove's letters from the fan letters, but he hadn't imagined someone else from Dry Creek would write to him. Just in case, he had given them Linda's name and Lance's name, but nothing had ever come from those two so it wasn't as though the letters he got were personal.

He couldn't even remember the last time he'd actually read one of his regular fan letters. The people who read his letters gave him reports, of course. He knew it was important to know what people wanted to tell him. That was his first indication of what songs people liked and what themes he should cover next.

"Sorry," Duane whispered. He had a feeling he would be saying that word a lot in his visit to Dry Creek. Did Lucy still think it was his home? That was kind of sweet. He wondered if anyone else here would claim him.

Duane barely even noticed that Phil had walked over to the table and sat down.

"They've taken the bait," Phil announced, with an edge of triumph in his voice. "A stringer from each of the four major magazines is coming. That's great. We've got them curious. All you've got to do now is—"

Duane held up his hand to silence Phil. He knew what they had to do, he just didn't want to see the look in the eyes of the people watching him when Phil said it all out loud and matter-of-fact as if the two of them did this sort of thing all the time. He figured there would be no hope the old men sitting here would ever respect him if they knew what he had planned.

In the past, Duane had figured giving the press something to say was just part of the game. He'd never thought about whether the words he and Phil said to the reporters were true. It was always about whether or not those words would get them more fans for the band. More fans meant more success. And success was what was important, wasn't it?

After all, no one expected the things they read in these fan magazines to be true, Duane told himself. Then he looked at Lucy's face. He guessed some people still did expect the words of Duane Enger to mean something.

"Out of here," Duane whispered to Phil as he stood up from the table. After seeing Lucy's face, Duane was afraid to even look at Linda. He didn't want to see the disapproval in her eyes.

In his years with the band, there had been many times when Duane had been less than sincere in his meetings with the press. Sometimes he'd endorse a product he knew wasn't any good, but he'd say it was good just because the company was the sponsor of a concert or something. That was the way things worked in the entertainment world.

When Duane opened the door, he realized he'd never lied in front of people who knew him as a person and not as a rock star. The people in Dry Creek might not care how things were in the big world. He had a feeling that none of those old men sitting inside would get up in front of a bunch of reporters and lie about how they felt about God, even if they were singing a tune when they were doing it.

Phil had grabbed a cup of coffee before he left the café and he handed it to Duane as they stood on the porch.

"What was that all about?" Phil asked as he handed the coffee to Duane. "Those people are going to hear what you're saying at some point anyway."

Duane nodded as he took the coffee. He knew that. He just needed to brace himself for it.

Phil was quiet for a minute as they walked down the café steps and headed back to their bus. "That's the woman, isn't it? Linda. The girl in that song. Your old high school sweetheart?"

Duane nodded as he took a gulp of the coffee.

Phil kept talking. "A woman like that doesn't come along all that often. Maybe you shouldn't have left her."

"I didn't leave her. She left me." The coffee was helping his voice once more so there was a little volume to his whisper.

"Oh." Phil paused in his walking to look at Duane. "Well, we can't let the reporters get hold of that little tidbit. Maybe you could talk to her and ask her not to mention anything about your relationship to them if anyone asks."

Duane grunted as he kept walking. "Believe me, she's not bragging about it anywhere."

Phil hurried to catch up. "Really? Most women would want to talk about rejecting the Jazz Man."

Now that was a depressing thought, Duane told himself. "Well, if Linda wants to say something about it, more power to her."

Phil didn't look too happy about that. "Maybe I should talk to her."

Duane shook his head. "Let her be."

Linda had watched the door close behind Duane and his manager before she turned to her sister.

"I'm sorry, sweetie." Linda stepped toward Lucy and opened her arms.

"He didn't write that letter." Lucy let herself be hugged. "You were right all along."

"I'm sure he would have written one if he'd even seen the letter from you," Linda said as she patted Lucy on the back. "I'm sure he gets too many letters to read them all by himself."

"I suppose." Lucy nodded.

The old men stood up from their tables.

"He's not so bad, maybe," Charley said as he started walking toward the door. He didn't look at Linda and Lucy, but he said it loud enough so they would hear. "Could be he'll turn out all right, given time."

Elmer grunted as he looked back at Charley. "Why would you say a fool thing like that?"

"Because I keep remembering Boots," Charley said as Elmer opened the door. "I've gotten acquainted with that dog since I've been at Mrs. Hargrove's so much, and I've never known a worthless boy or man to raise a dog like Boots."

Linda figured that wasn't much to go on, but she didn't say anything as the men walked out the door.

"At least we didn't name the café after him," Lucy said as she left Linda's arms and walked over to the wall where the guitar hung.

"He's only human, Luce," Linda said, using the nickname she had for her sister. She never thought she would be defending Duane to Lucy.

Lucy reached over and took the framed letter off the wall. She put it facedown on a nearby table.

Linda wished she had more to say to her sister. Sometimes, though, disappointments just had to work themselves out. Things were not always what people thought they were; that was just part of life.

Now that Linda thought about it, Duane didn't look the way she had expected him to look, either. She knew he was sick, but beyond that he didn't look happy. The Duane she remembered wasn't the smiling type, but he was always passionate about something. He used to look so alive, even if he was filled with thunderstorms instead of sunshine. He wasn't that way anymore. If anything, he looked tepid. Maybe his life wasn't lived as fully as she imagined, after all.

Just then Mrs. Hargrove came into the café. The older woman was wearing a blue gingham housedress that zipped up the front and a new pair of white orthopedic shoes. She was supposed to use a rubber-tipped walking cane when the ground was muddy, but Linda noticed the older woman didn't have it with her.

"I came as soon as I heard," Mrs. Hargrove said, looking around the café. "Did he leave already?"

Linda didn't need to ask who Mrs. Hargrove was looking for.

"I think he went back to the bus with his manager."

"They're not leaving town yet, are they?"

Linda shook her head. "They're pretty stuck in the mud there. Right in the driveway to Duane's great-aunt's place. I don't know how they'll get that bus out. Besides, Duane's making plans to sing a song in church next Sunday."

"Well, isn't that nice!"

Mrs. Hargrove started to beam.

Linda started to frown. "I don't think it's nice." Linda lowered her voice so Lucy couldn't hear what she was saying. "Duane's only singing that song so he can get some publicity. I heard his manager talking on the phone and that's what they're planning. The two of them are planning to make a mockery of God, right here in Dry Creek."

Mrs. Hargrove smiled. "It's not that easy to do, you know. Making a mockery of God. The good Lord sometimes turns the tables on people."

"Well, I hope He turns them on Duane." Linda regretted the words as soon as they were out of her mouth. Fortunately, Lucy didn't look as though she had heard. Linda turned to the older woman. "That doesn't sound very nice, does it? I suppose I should pray for his soul instead of letting him upset me. I find it's not always so easy to be very understanding."

Linda wondered if she'd ever become the kind of Christian that Mrs. Hargrove was. Nothing seemed to make the older woman turn on another person. It was discouraging for Linda to realize that her old hurts and resentments were so close to the surface and could make her wish hard times for someone else.

"Of course, I don't want anything *really* bad to happen to Duane," Linda added. At least, she could say that much for herself. She drew the line at death and serious disease.

"Oh, it won't hurt the boy to squirm," Mrs. Hargrove said as she gave Linda a hug. "I'd be surprised if people haven't started being too easy on him anyway now that he's a star."

The hug made Linda feel much better. "And he's meeting with Pastor Curtis so he won't be able to get away with too much."

Mrs. Hargrove nodded. "I think our Pastor Curtis will know just how to handle your Duane. Don't you worry."

"He's not *my* Duane," Linda said, but Mrs. Hargrove was already walking over toward Lucy. Linda hoped no one was under the impression that she and Duane were anything anymore.

Oh. A thought stopped her cold. She had forgotten.

She and Duane were still something. Until she paid him back the money he'd used in the start-up of the diner, they were probably still legally business partners. She didn't have the money in the kitchen, of course. The coffee can back there only held about eighty dollars. She had the money in her savings account in Miles City, though, or at least she hoped she did. She'd taken some out to pay for Lucy's last dentist bill. She hoped she still had enough to pay Duane off. She didn't want to owe the man anything, even if it meant she never got that jukebox for her café.

Chapter Five

Duane sat on a wooden chair in Pastor Curtis's office. He'd left his shoes outside the church sanctuary. It had started to drizzle and his walk back into town from the bus had been muddy. He could feel the cold of the floor through his socks and his T-shirt was damp.

It was one o'clock and his meeting with the pastor was just beginning. Fortunately there was a nice steady heat coming from the register on the wall of the church office.

"Sorry about Phil," Duane said. He was as nervous as if he were facing a roomful of hostile reporters. He'd found some old cough drops in the bus and he'd been sucking on them. They seemed to work better than the coffee had for his voice. He had one in his mouth now.

"Oh, don't worry about it. I just have a policy of meeting with people one-on-one, for the first time at least. I'm happy to meet with Phil later. In fact, I could call him now and set something up."

Pastor Curtis reached for the phone that sat on the old desk next to the chair he was sitting in. Duane was glad the pastor hadn't seated himself behind that big executive desk. It was a lot more friendly just to have the two of them sitting around this coffee table.

"No, no," Duane said. "Phil's good with just me being here. I'm the one who needs to sing the song anyway."

Duane gave his performance smile; the one that worked with the press.

The pastor only nodded as he put back the phone. "I guess that's true. Have you decided what song to sing?"

"Oh." This was the first time that Duane realized he hadn't given any thought to what he would sing. He'd worried about where to place the microphone so it wouldn't seem that he was taking the place of the pastor in the pulpit but would still have him standing where everyone could see him. He'd looked through his shirts to be sure he had a white shirt to wear under the blue choir robe. It needed to be washed, but it was there. "I suppose I should sing something…ah…religious."

Duane knew he sounded clueless, but it didn't seem to bother Pastor Curtis.

"Often our soloists like to pick a song that says something about their relationship with God."

"Ah—" Duane wondered if his voice would leave him. He had to swallow twice to get enough air to speak. He certainly had no relationship with God so that was no help. "I thought…I mean…doesn't the church have a book of songs?"

"A hymnal? Sure. That's a good place to start." Pastor Curtis stood up. "I'll bring one in. Do you want something to drink? I have some cold sodas in the refrigerator. Sorry, I didn't make any coffee today."

"Soda would be good," Duane managed to say.

The pastor left the room and Duane slumped down in his chair. He was doomed. This business about singing in the church was going to turn bad. He could feel it in his bones. If he wasn't so polite, he would slip out the back door of the church and make a run for it back to the bus. Of course, he didn't have his shoes and he'd look crazy running across the mud in his socks.

And even when he reached the bus, where would he go? He was stuck. Everyone in Dry Creek knew where to find him. If the pastor didn't track him down, someone else would. And then he'd have to explain why he was uncomfortable, all of which would make him even more uneasy.

The pastor came back with a couple of navy-blue books and a can of soda.

"Sorry I don't have much choice of flavors," the pastor said as he handed the soda to Duane. "I think my boys have been by."

The pastor glanced over at the picture on his desk of two twin boys around nine years old. The satisfied love on his face was unmistakable. "I forgot I told them they could have a can if they helped pick up trash around town."

Duane nodded as he opened the top of the can. "Good boys."

The pastor nodded. "They *are* good boys. Full of energy and mischief, but they've never met someone who they didn't want to befriend."

Duane put the soda can to his lips and took a long drink. He wondered if those boys knew how lucky they were to have a father that felt that way about them.

Duane had never even known his father. It had just been him and his mother and sometimes that man Pete, until he was sent to Great-Aunt Cornelia.

"Well," the pastor said as he handed one of the hymnals to Duane. "Why don't you look for a minute? It could be anything. How merciful you find God. How much you want to dry worship Him. What your life was like before you gave yourself to Him."

"Ahh…" Duane squirmed as he opened the book. "Isn't there something smaller?"

"Smaller?"

Duane nodded. "Yeah, maybe something that mentions His kindness to animals or how nice the stars look at night. You know, something less—"

"Personal," Pastor Curtis added when Duane seemed stuck.

"Yeah." Duane was relieved. "Something that's more, well, general."

"Do you have any favorite hymns?"

Duane shook his head. "I don't really know much about hymns."

Pastor Curtis was silent at that.

Finally, Duane couldn't stand it. "I mean, we're getting the reporters here because they think I have something to say about God and me, but I don't. Not really. I know nothing about Him."

Duane knew Phil would want him to swear the pastor to secrecy on that point, but Duane figured they would just have to cope with any fallout that came if the pastor started to talk. Pastor Curtis seemed like a decent sort of person anyway; he wasn't likely to tattle.

"Well, that's a good start," Pastor Curtis said with satisfaction. "God can always work in a humble heart. I was there myself before I turned back to the Lord."

"Oh." Duane was startled. "Oh, no, I don't want—"

Pastor Curtis held up his hand. "Relax. You don't have to worry. I was just going to suggest that you take the hymnal and read through fifty or so hymns. Get to know God and then we'll talk some more. How about Monday?"

"I guess I could do that."

"And there's church tomorrow at eleven. Right here. I'll see that we sing lots of hymns. You won't want to miss it. It'll give you some ideas. Besides, your old friend Lance will be giving his testimony."

Duane sat up straight. "Lance Walker?"

The pastor nodded.

"Well," Duane said and then swallowed. That was about all he could say in front of the pastor. What would possess Lance to talk in church? "Is he asking for money or something? Lance?"

The last Duane had heard Lance was riding some rodeo and working on the Elkton Ranch. Maybe he'd hurt himself and needed help. The life of a ranch hand wasn't very secure and the church had these benevolence offerings. That was one thing Duane had paid attention to when he had gone to church with his great-aunt. He understood hard times and he was glad people were getting what they needed.

Duane was reaching for his wallet when the pastor smiled. "No, it's not about money. Lance is going to talk about meeting God and what that's meant for his life."

Duane hoped that wasn't pious talk for Lance announcing his intention to get married or something like that. Lance had probably had a crush on Linda all through high school and Duane just hadn't noticed.

Duane couldn't ask the pastor about Lance and Linda, though, so he just stood up. It was suddenly clear. He never should have come back to Dry Creek. He had a bad feeling he was going to find out things he didn't want to know. A lot of time had passed since he'd been here last.

"And bring Phil to church with you," Pastor Curtis said as he also stood and held out his hand to Duane. "Welcome home to Dry Creek, by the way."

"Thanks," Duane said as he shook the pastor's hand.

Duane walked back through the sanctuary to get to the front door of the church. He and Phil had already visited the sanctuary, but that was to plan where to put the lights and the sound equipment.

Duane realized he hadn't really looked at the inside of the church since he'd come back until now. This was the place where Linda went to services and Lance was going to speak tomorrow. It was the place where he'd sat with Great-Aunt Cornelia and wondered when the preacher would stop talking. This new pastor hadn't been in the pulpit back then. Not that it would probably have made much difference to Duane. He wouldn't have listened anyway.

Duane had a sudden longing to be back sitting beside Great-Aunt Cornelia in the pew that was the third from the front. His great-aunt always sat in the same place, with him right next to her. He wished she was still alive.

Duane walked around. There was a chart on one wall that showed the weekly Sunday school attendance. There was a slow growth upward, but still the highest number was ninety-five. A mural of a mountain was painted on the wall behind the pulpit and a handmade banner hung to one side, proclaiming Jesus Loves Me.

Duane smiled for the first time since he'd come into this church. That was the one song he remembered from his childhood. He sat down on one of the pews and gave himself over to memories. He remembered Mrs. Hargrove as his Sunday school teacher. Great-Aunt Cornelia had pressed him to go to Sunday school and Mrs. Hargrove had taken over. They'd sung the "Jesus Loves Me" song every week for months in her class when she found out that he would sing it. Of course, he didn't believe it, but the words were simple and, for some reason, he could remember the words to that one.

He hadn't been in Dry Creek for even a year when Lance showed up in town. He was staying with old man Higgins, doing odd chores for the man in exchange for room and board. Mr. Higgins was one of the few people in Dry Creek who didn't go to church, but Lance must have been curious about the place because he started tormenting Duane and teasing him about what went on behind the closed church doors when everyone was inside.

Duane had never paid much attention to things and he didn't like to be questioned, so he never really answered Lance's questions. Who would have thought Lance would end up part of this church? He must have decided to get his own answers to the questions he had as a boy.

Duane opened the hymnal. He might as well read a few of those hymns right now. It was peaceful in here. Besides, he could see through the one window that was opened and the sky was heavy gray outside. He was in no hurry to walk back to the bus if it was going to rain.

Duane had read through several hymns when he heard a soft whine coming from the front door of the church. It sounded familiar so he got up and went to the door.

"Boots!"

Duane knelt down. Good old Boots had found Duane's shoes and was guarding them, lying on the church steps with his tail thumping. Boots stood up when he saw Duane and cocked his head to the side as though not sure if he was seeing right.

"Yeah, it's me. How're you doing, old boy?" Duane buried his face in Boots's hair. They both smelled of wet dog now. "I've missed you."

The two things Duane had taken everywhere as a boy in Dry Creek were his guitar and his dog.

Boots whined again and Duane scratched his hair. Boots was black all over except for his feet, which were white, more white in the front than in the back but high enough all around to earn his name.

"Duane!"

Duane looked up. "Mrs. Hargrove!"

The older woman stood at the bottom of the steps smiling.

Duane got on his feet and took the stairs down two at a time. He had his arms around the older woman before he remembered he must smell of wet dog.

He pulled back. "Sorry, I was just hugging Boots."

"A little dog hair never worried me," Mrs. Hargrove said as she stepped back a little. "Just let me look at you. I couldn't believe it when Charley called to say you were here."

"It was a spur-of-the-moment thing," Duane said. For the first time since he'd driven into Dry Creek, he felt welcome here. First Boots and now Mrs. Hargrove.

"I figured it must have been sudden since you didn't write."

"I've been on tour."

"Well, you'll have to tell me all 'bout it," Mrs. Hargrove said as she took Duane's arm. "But, look, it's starting to drizzle again. Come on over to the café and I'll buy you a cup of coffee."

"I don't think I can drink more coffee," Duane said. "It keeps my voice going, but I've already had five cups."

"What you need is some hot water with honey and lemon then," Mrs. Hargrove said as they started walking across the street. "It'll make you feel better in no time."

Duane followed the older woman and Boots followed them both.

"I hope something makes my voice better," Duane said. "I have to sing a week from Sunday."

Mrs. Hargrove stopped in the middle of the street and smiled at him proudly. "Yes, I heard. In church."

Duane would rather have faced God than Mrs. Hargrove on this. "It's not—I mean, I'm singing in church, but I'm just trying to be respectful of others' beliefs. I don't—you know—myself."

"I know," Mrs. Hargrove said calmly as she kept walking to the café. "You would have told me if you'd decided to mend your fences with God."

Duane relaxed. He thought that had gone pretty well. If Mrs. Hargrove was okay with him singing in church when he didn't exactly believe, then God would be okay with it, too. Duane decided he had just been too sensitive on the issue. After all, people sang love songs and that didn't mean they were in love. People sang about dying and that did not mean they were dead. A singer didn't have to mean every single word in a song to make it a worthwhile performance.

Duane sat the hymnal down on a table in the café and turned to look at Boots. His dog was standing there with his head cocked to one side as if he were asking a question. Boots had always been a smart dog.

"I don't have anything to use to tie him to the porch rail," Duane said as Linda came out of the café kitchen.

"As long as he stays on that rug beside the door, he's fine. That's where he stays when he comes in with Mrs. Hargrove."

Boots lay down on the rug, looking as though he had understood every word Linda had said.

Duane sat down at the table with Mrs. Hargrove.

"Do you have time to join us for some hot tea?" Mrs. Hargrove looked up at Linda. "Duane needs some hot water for his throat."

Linda nodded and looked at Duane. "I noticed you were hoarse. I hope it's getting better."

Duane marveled that she could say the words with so little warmth. "Thank you."

He watched Linda walk back to the kitchen. He could still tell when she was mad just by the way she moved. She seemed to put a little extra pressure into each step. Maybe she was picturing stomping on him each time her shoe hit the floor.

"I don't know why she's so upset," Duane muttered, almost to himself. "She's the one who said we wouldn't 'suit.' That was the word she used. That we wouldn't suit. It sounded like she'd copied her note out of an etiquette book."

"It was a hard time for her," Mrs. Hargrove said. "Her mother had just died. She was wondering how she was going to make a life for Lucy."

"I know," Duane said. "That's why I didn't press her on it. I thought she just needed some time. But then when I came here—"

Duane didn't know why he was dragging all of those old feelings out. He'd thought Linda would have decided to marry someone else by now anyway. For all of those years, he'd been waiting for someone to tell him she'd gotten married. He'd never pictured her with Lance, but he'd thought she'd be with someone steady, sort of a *Father Knows Best* kind of a man. The problem was that Lance didn't know any more about being a husband than Duane did. It didn't seem fair that he would lose her to Lance.

Mrs. Hargrove nodded. "I know. She wouldn't see you."

"She told you that?" Duane said, suddenly alert again. He didn't think Linda had gone around telling people she wouldn't see him back then.

"She didn't have to tell me. It was obvious."

"I suppose I looked pretty bad that time I was here last."

"So did she."

The door to the kitchen opened and Linda stepped back into the main room of the café. She was carrying a tray with three steaming cups and a metal bowl of something.

"I heated some water for Boots, too," Linda said as she set the tray on the table and picked up the metal bowl. "And added a little milk to make it interesting."

Linda knelt down and put the metal bowl on the rug beside Boots. She petted the dog before she stood back up. Duane thought he'd never seen a prettier sight than Linda petting Boots.

"There's some honey on the counter," Linda said as she sat down at the table and wiped her hands with some disinfectant cream she had on the tray. Then she slid the cup of plain hot water over to Duane. "There's some lemon slices there, too, left from yesterday. I've already used the ones I cut this morning for the tea orders."

Duane nodded as he got to his feet. In other words, he was on his own. He took his cup of hot water with him to the counter.

He heard Linda asking Mrs. Hargrove if she wanted a little cold water in her tea to make it just right. Or maybe a little cream.

"I know you like the raw sugar," Linda said as she offered a small dish of it to the older woman.

"I'm not contagious," Duane said when he sat back down at the table with his honey and lemon and hot water. He started to squeeze the slices of lemon. They'd sat for so long that most of the juice had already drained out. But he squeezed what juice he could into the hot water; he knew better than to ask for a fresh slice.

"You should have a doctor look at your throat," Linda said calmly as she poured her own tea. "You won't be able to sing if your voice stays like that."

Duane nodded as he spooned some honey out of the jar. "Two doctors have already looked."

He put the spoon of honey in his hot water.

Linda suddenly looked up from her tea with the first honest emotion on her face that Duane had seen since he came. Linda was panicked. "What would we do with all of those reporters if you can't do your solo? Isn't that what they'll all be here for—that and a press conference afterward?" Linda turned to him. "They'd be all over town looking for something else to write about if you don't come through."

Duane didn't need to ask Linda what she was worried about. She was worried that, if the reporters started really digging, someone would lead them straight to her. His sweetheart.

"Well, we'll just have to see that Duane is able to sing," Mrs. Hargrove said calmly. "Maybe he should get someone to help him sing."

Duane started to smile. "I could use someone to sing with me. It would take some of the strain off my voice. I'd have no problem if I had some help."

"You used to sing with Duane," Mrs. Hargrove said as she turned to Linda. "Maybe you could help him out."

"Oh, no, I—" Linda started to say.

Duane didn't let her finish. "I'll pay you."

"Pay me?"

Linda and Mrs. Hargrove both looked astonished.

"To sing in church?"

Duane nodded. "In church with me, of course."

"Oh, I couldn't—" Linda started again.

"How much?" Mrs. Hargrove was the one to interrupt this time.

Linda turned to the older woman in surprise. "You can't seriously think—"

Mrs. Hargrove put a hand on Linda's arm and turned to her. "You were just telling me you were planning to take money out of your savings account. Maybe you won't need to take as much."

"Yes, but—"

"She can name her price," Duane said.

Well, that stopped all of the conversation, Duane thought to himself. Linda was staring at him now as if he'd grown a second head. Even Mrs. Hargrove looked startled. It took a moment for anyone to say anything.

"Twelve hundred dollars," Linda finally announced.

Duane hoped he got the bus dug out soon. He'd have to make a trip into Miles City since that was probably where the nearest bank was. He had a few hundred in cash with him, but he didn't have twelve hundred dollars. When he said she could name her price, he was thinking in the low hundreds. "We're not selling tickets to my performance, you know. It's just at the end of the church service. It's free for everyone."

Linda nodded. "I know. I want to pay back what you put into the café when we started."

"Oh, but that's already water under the bridge," Duane said. "You don't need to worry about that."

"I don't need charity," Linda said.

"It's not charity," Duane said. "I made an investment in the café. I never expected to get it back."

"I insist on paying you back."

"You can pay me back in your will."

"I don't have a will."

"Well, you should have one with Lucy and all." Duane wondered if he should put the two of them in his will. Someone needed to think about Lucy's future. And he already had more money than he would need in his lifetime.

"I'm working on it," Linda said. "But I'm not going to wait to pay you back. I'm going to do it as soon as I can. And, that's the price I'm charging to sing with you. Take it or leave it. If I help you, the money goes to repaying the money you put into the business. Otherwise, I don't have time to sing with you. I'll be too busy running my café and hoping to make some money that way."

Duane nodded. This wasn't like the old Linda he used to know and he approved. It took a little grit to survive in life. Besides, he would take any deal she offered. He needed a friend when he stood up there in church and sang. Not that Linda was still his friend, but she had been once. Maybe the memory of their friendship would be enough.

Chapter Six

Linda put earrings on as she got ready to go to church. She was standing at the counter in the bathroom putting on makeup and jewelry. The door was open and she could hear Lucy getting dressed.

Linda hadn't worn earrings much of late and she wanted to wear something to make herself feel a little more dressed up than usual. Duane probably already thought she was hopelessly out of style, but she wanted to look as good as she could since she hadn't bought a new dress for five years.

She could have bought a dress, Linda told herself as she combed through her hair again. It's just that—with one thing and another—it always seemed that something else was more important, like a new coffeepot for the café or braces for Lucy.

Linda looked over as her sister entered the bathroom to stand in front of the mirror with her. "You're not wearing that to church. You've outgrown that dress, that's why it's so short."

"I don't have anything else to wear," Lucy complained as she opened the drawer where she kept her makeup. "Everything else in my closet is so lame."

"There's nothing lame about that brown and turquoise blouse you have. It looks great with those pants I got you."

"But this dress makes me look older." Lucy pulled out a tube of mascara.

Linda looked at her sister. "Trust me. You're not going to look older until we agree you're ready for it. That blouse is perfectly fine for a fifteen-year-old girl."

Lucy leaned closer to the mirror to put on some mascara. "When you were my age, I bet you were wearing miniskirts that were even shorter than this."

Linda saw no need to tell Lucy that the reason Linda watched her sister's clothes so carefully was because no one had cared what Linda wore. She could have walked down the street with her neckline plunging to her navel and her mother wouldn't have even noticed. In fact, Linda thought later that she had dressed the way she had as a pathetic attempt to get her mother's attention as much as she had been trying to get the attention of the boys. She was lucky Duane's scowls had kept the other boys away from her. Nothing had brought her mother's attention to her.

"When I was your age, I was walking to school," Linda said with a smile for her sister. "In the snow. Pulling a sled to carry all my books. All twenty pounds of them. And a dictionary, too. In small print and me with my secondhand glasses."

Lucy set the mascara down and smiled. The school story was an old joke with them. "All right, so don't tell me about the miniskirts. I bet the Jazz Man remembers."

"You are not to ask Duane Enger about my skirts."

"We'll see," Lucy teased.

Linda wasn't sure if it was a good thing or not that her sister had seemed to forgive Duane for not reading her letter. Lucy had apparently decided that music stars have their own rules that told them what to do and, if Duane had decided not to read any letters, that it was an okay decision because he was famous. Linda would have to talk to her sister about that sometime soon. No one was above the rules of politeness, not even the most famous person in the world. And that, definitely, was not the Jazz Man.

Duane kept looking down the street as he stood at the bottom of the stairs leading into the church. The sky was gray and it was going to start raining any second now. He could smell the dampness. But he'd almost rather stand in the rain than go inside the church. He'd already shaken hands with a dozen of Dry Creek's finest citizens and he was no more comfortable about all of this than he had been when he first came to this church seventeen years ago. A man like him just didn't belong in church. There was no elbow room. He didn't even know why he'd come this morning.

Then he saw the Morgan car pull into a spot in front of the church and he knew exactly why he'd come. He watched Linda and her sister get out of the car.

He'd do a lot more than go to church to see Linda.

Linda had her hair pulled back into a twist and silver hoops on her ears. She wore a navy skirt and a baggy sweater knit from natural yarn. It was a far cry from the clothes she used to wear. Nothing clashed or sparkled or revealed too much. It was all very tame. Somehow, in the years when he had been gone, Linda had grown up. It didn't seem fair. He felt that he'd missed out on something. And, all this time, he'd thought he'd had it all.

"Nice day," Duane said when Linda and Lucy reached the steps.

Lucy gave him a shy smile, but it seemed Linda was going to march right on by without greeting him.

"Yes." Linda managed to stop long enough to reply. "The coolness is refreshing."

Duane smiled. Once Linda started taking to him, he had a chance. His voice was much better now and he believed he could recapture some of the feelings she used to have for him if he could only talk to her long enough.

"Nice outfit," Duane said as he started walking up the stairs on the left side of Linda.

Lucy was on the right of Linda and had to look around her sister to talk to him. "Don't you think the skirt's too long? It makes her look old."

"Lucy!" Linda said.

Duane smiled. "Your sister looks great in anything she wears. Always has. Always will."

Linda turned pink and Duane chose to believe it was because she was flustered instead of angry.

"We're going to be late if we don't get inside and get seated," Linda said as she took the last step up the stairs and reached for the church door.

Linda was trapped by her good manners. Duane had followed her and Lucy into the church and down the

aisle. She supposed it seemed natural for him to sit
beside them, but she wished he wouldn't have done so.
She didn't need anyone in Dry Creek speculating about
what it meant that he was sitting next to her.

For the first time in her life, she wished there was
assigned seating in church. Alphabetical maybe. At least
then Duane wouldn't be anywhere near her.

"You don't need to sit so close," Linda finally whispered to him. He was inching closer and closer to her.
"There's plenty of room."

Duane looked at her in surprise. "Sorry."

Great, Linda thought. Now he knows I'm bothered
by the fact that he's sitting so close and he wasn't even
aware of how close we were.

When he reached over and pulled a hymnal from the
rack, she was mortified further. He hadn't even been
trying to sit close to her; he'd just been trying to get a
hymnal. She wished she could hide under the pew.

"You smell of lemon," she finally said. "Your voice?"

Duane nodded again.

Linda was relieved when the service began and
Lance was called up to speak. At least that would take
Duane's attention completely away from her. Not that
it was on her to begin with.

Duane had never been so glad to see a cup of coffee
as he was at the end of that church service. He'd played
hooky from church as often as he could those last few
years in Dry Creek because Lance had convinced him
church was for sissies and now, right up there in the
pulpit, he had seen Lance cry. Oh, maybe tears hadn't
rolled down the man's cheeks or anything, but Duane

knew Lance well enough to know the man was blinking back the tears.

The whole world had gone upside-down crazy.

Lance wasn't supposed to cry about anything. He had always been tougher in some ways than Duane. The man was part Sioux warrior, after all. When Duane would yell as he'd done on the streets of Chicago, Lance would turn stoic like his forefathers. There wasn't a soft spot in Lance's heart, unless it was for some rodeo horse somewhere. And, yet, Lance had teared up when he told everyone how much he owed God for saving him from himself.

A man like Lance wasn't supposed to need anyone. And, if he did, it would be because he'd come up against a grizzly bear or a woolly mammoth or a war party from a different tribe. He didn't need help coming up against *himself*.

It didn't take much to see where Lance's talk was leading, either, not when all of the women in the church were pulling out their handkerchiefs and dabbing at their eyes. If Lance thought God had saved him, he hadn't seen anything yet. Where God left off, the women of Dry Creek would take over.

Lance would be married within a year. Duane could see it all now. What was making his blood run cold was that Linda had been the one the older women in the church had kept looking at as Lance walked down from the pulpit.

Duane drained the last of his coffee from the cup and looked around.

There was a tub of empty coffee cups on the counter

over there. Once he put his cup in, he would be free to leave.

He could see Linda and Lucy over in a corner of the church foyer talking to Mrs. Hargrove. He wouldn't put it past them all to be planning a wedding between Linda and Lance right now. Women were always such suckers for a sob story.

Duane growled. Lance was standing off to his right talking to the older men that seemed to hang around Linda's place.

Then Lance looked right over at him and Duane paled. He had no desire to talk to the testimony guy while the holy glow was still on his face. Duane wasn't fast enough, though. Lance met up with him at the tub with the empty cups.

"Just putting my cup away," Duane said.

"I never answered your postcards," Lance said.

What was it with the people of Dry Creek and letters? "They were nothing. Honest. Forget about it."

Lance threw his arm around Duane and hugged him close. "I'm sorry, pal."

Duane would rather have Lance wrestle him to the ground than hug him. "You don't need to be sorry. It's okay. I get free postcards from the band anyway. It's just that I'd said I'd write and—"

Lance kept him locked in a hug until Duane thought maybe the other man did intend to wrestle him. Or at least squeeze him to death.

He saw Linda's sweater even though he couldn't see all of her because she was standing behind Lance and Duane swore the other man almost had him in a headlock.

"You said you'd write me, too," Linda said.

And with that, Lance let Duane go.

"I'll see you two later," Lance said as he backed away from Duane. "Mrs. Hargrove wants to give me something."

Lance always had been a coward when it came to women, Duane told himself.

"I didn't think you'd want a letter," Duane said. He was no braver than Lance even if he talked with more women. Still, some things needed to be said. "You said you didn't want to go with me on the road. I wanted you to come."

"But you knew I couldn't," Linda hissed back. "You knew I had Lucy."

Duane saw Lucy before Linda did. The younger girl had come up behind Linda with a smile on her face and a white piece of paper in her hand. It didn't take long to realize Lucy had heard them.

"I'll come back," Lucy whispered. Her face was stricken. "I just thought—"

"Lucy," Linda said as she turned around.

Lucy waved the piece of paper. "I just wanted his real signature on the letter. That's all."

"Lucy, I didn't mean… It's not like—"

Duane took an instinctive step closer to Linda. She suddenly looked frail.

Lucy walked away quickly and Linda let her go.

Linda turned to him. "How could you tell her something like that?"

"Didn't she know I wanted you to come with me?"

"Of course not," Linda snapped at him. "That's not the kind of thing I'd tell my baby sister."

"Hey, it wasn't like that. We were going to get married. We would have been respectable."

"There's nothing respectable about the life of a rock star," Linda protested. "At least, nothing stable. How would we have managed? With school? And friends? I couldn't have Lucy hanging around with the band members. There might have even been drugs. She was only seven."

Now it was Linda blinking back tears.

Duane noticed that the room had grown quiet. There were no conversations in the corners. Everyone was looking at the two of them.

"Here, let's go find Lucy," Duane said as he put his arm around Linda and started them toward the door. He'd forgotten how everyone knew a person's business when they were in a small town. Not that it mattered to him. But it probably mattered to Linda. That's the only reason he didn't stop and kiss her. He'd never realized the burdens she'd carried years ago when she came to see him in Hollywood.

"You don't need to sign her letter," Linda said as they walked to the door. "I know you get lots of letters."

"Sometimes I don't get enough," Duane said. "Especially not ones from Dry Creek."

Duane wondered suddenly. "You never wrote me, did you?"

"Me?" Linda looked surprised. "Of course not."

"Oh."

"I had nothing to say."

Duane smiled. "I guess it was just me then that didn't know what was going on."

"What do you mean?"

"I always thought you left because you didn't want to be with me. I never knew it was all of these things with Lucy. We could have worked those things out."

"Well, it's too late for that now," Linda said.

Duane couldn't bring himself to nod in agreement, even though he knew it was true. Not for the reasons Linda thought. He was the reason it wouldn't work out. Seeing Linda and Lucy again made him realize his failings even more. He just didn't know enough about being a husband or a family man. Maybe, if Linda had gone with him years ago, he'd have been selfish enough to let her come. But not now. He knew better now. He felt sadder than he'd ever felt before just thinking about the chance he'd missed.

Linda found Lucy in the car. Her younger sister was sitting in the passenger side of the vehicle, looking straight ahead.

"You don't need to hurry for me," Lucy said as Linda opened the door. "I'm fine with waiting."

"Lucy," Linda started. "Look at me."

Her sister turned.

"I love you," Linda said. "I will admit I was a bit unprepared for parenthood when our mother died, but you have been my light and joy."

"I stopped you from going away with Duane."

"Duane stopped me from going away with Duane. Or maybe it was God," Linda said. "All I know is that he and I weren't ready to be married back then and I wouldn't have gone with him unless we did marry. Besides, he was going off to make a name for himself and I—" Linda smiled "—well, I had much more important things to do."

"I'm sorry," Lucy said as she wiped away a tear.

"Ah, Luce," Linda said as she hugged her sister to her as best as she could in the car. "What would I do without you?"

"You would have been the Jazz Man's wife."

Linda frowned. "Now who would want to have a title like that? People would call me Mrs. Jazz Man. Like Mrs. Potato Head."

Lucy giggled.

"Besides," Linda said as she released Lucy and put her hands on the wheel. "We would have missed out on all of these years in Dry Creek. This is our home. Not everyone is so blessed to have a circle of friends like we do."

Lucy nodded. "I think Duane is lonely."

"If he is, it's by choice," Linda said as she turned the ignition on her car.

Linda had wondered many times if Duane had a girlfriend or even a wife who hadn't been made public. She suspected rock stars weren't always honest about their home life if a wife would make them less appealing to fans. For all she knew, he might even have someone now. There was nothing that said he had to be more honest with the people of Dry Creek than he was with his fans.

"He's a pathetic excuse for a man," Linda muttered to herself.

"Who?" Lucy asked.

"Never mind," Linda said. She didn't want Lucy to worry about the character of Duane.

Linda concentrated on driving. The roads weren't as slippery since the rain had eased up somewhat, but she could still get the car stuck if she didn't watch herself. If Duane did have a wife, Linda pitied the poor woman. It couldn't be easy living in that bus with all of the band members. At least she knew the band members were all male. She did keep up with things that much.

"There. We're home," Linda said with satisfaction. The house had never been much. It was a two-story frame house built in 1935. But she and Lucy had managed to put a new coat of white paint on it last year and she had flowers planted all around the edge of the house. In a few weeks, the house would be blooming with a colorful trim.

The house hadn't always belonged to Linda. It was actually her uncle's house and she'd bought it from a cousin when her uncle had died. Morgans had lived here for decades, though, and she and Lucy had settled into the house with their mother about the time their mother had gotten sick.

Linda looked around the yard before she stepped out of the car. There was nothing fancy around. There were some pine trees to the west and a couple of sheds to the east that housed some farm equipment her uncle had used. Linda had leased the farmland out that went around the house, but she thought that someday she and Lucy might grow wheat or something so she kept the equipment. Last summer they had grown a big garden and they'd planted more blackberry bushes. They were still using those berries in their pies.

They had a good life here, Linda told herself. She'd known that before Duane came back, but thinking about what her life might have been like reminded her of it even more firmly. She had made the right choice to raise Lucy here.

"I wonder if Duane has ever been to Paris?" Lucy asked as Linda opened the door to their house. "Wouldn't that be something?"

Linda only grunted and reminded herself that no seven-year-old girl had ever needed to see Paris. The fact that Lucy might enjoy the travel at her present age didn't mean it would have been as welcome back then.

"I don't know if he made it to Europe," Linda said as she stepped into the house. "I heard his band is on their way to Puerto Vallarta though."

Linda saw no need to tell Lucy that the band was traveling in a private yacht.

"I think there's lots of insects in Puerto Vallarta," Linda said instead as she walked to the kitchen. "Huge monster ones."

"Oh." Lucy frowned. "Do you think they bite?"

"Probably," Linda said cheerfully as she turned a knob on the oven. "Now, get changed and help me get dinner on the table."

Linda doubted Duane ever had meat loaf anymore. He probably dined on filet mignon and sushi. Or maybe even Russian caviar. Served with imported cheese from the mountains of Switzerland.

Chapter Seven

Duane looked at the open can of sardines Phil was holding out to him. Duane had walked back from church without thinking about food. He'd thought about how fast the ground underneath him was drying out and wondered when he'd be able to gun the motor on the bus hard enough to get it unstuck, but he hadn't thought about what he was going to eat for Sunday dinner.

"That's all I found in the cupboard," Phil said as he looked down at the can in his hands mournfully. "I think they're left from that costume party last—when was that anyway?"

Duane frowned. "Aren't these sardines what we were going to smash up to make into monster brains?"

Duane wondered when he had been that young. It must have been three or four years ago. He wondered what other odd things were rolling around in this bus.

Phil shrugged. "Well, it's all we have. Except for three more cans of the same. Two apiece. What kind of a place is this Dry Creek anyway where the café closes on Sunday? Don't they know people have to eat? We've been all over in this bus and we've always been able to eat."

"Everything closes on Sunday here," Duane said. He should have thought of the implications of that earlier in the day. Dry Creek wasn't like other places. They didn't have traffic lights and they didn't have businesses that were open on Sunday.

Phil grunted. "I bet no one else in town is eating sardines."

Duane looked down at the greasy fish and sighed. "No, I don't expect they are."

He didn't want to torture Phil with his guesses as to what the dinner tables around Dry Creek held today but, if his memory served him right, Mrs. Hargrove would have roast beef with mashed potatoes and the cook out at the Elkton Ranch would be grilling steaks about now. Even Elmer Maynard would probably be dishing himself up a bowl of his famous white bean and ham soup.

Duane also didn't see any need to mention that he'd been so upset after his conversation with Linda and Lucy that he'd turned down Sunday dinner invitations from both Mrs. Hargrove and some of the hands at the Elkton ranch. He could probably have even thrown a hint Elmer's way and gotten an invitation for soup. At the time, Duane hadn't thought of the significance of those invitations.

He was thinking of it now though. "I thought we had some dried Cup-a-Soup packages somewhere. Wasn't it chicken noodle?"

Phil flushed pink. "Well, there was breakfast, you

know. The café wasn't open for that, either. And I knew you were having coffee and doughnuts at church."

"There were doughnuts?" Duane wondered how he could have missed those. It seemed Lance could have mentioned the doughnuts when he was giving Duane that bear hug and going on about postcards. "I suppose they're long gone by now."

Both men just stood in the shadows of the bus and looked at those sardines.

"If we had some transportation, we could go over to Linda's place," Phil finally said. "She used to be sweet on you."

"Used to be," Duane agreed. "But that doesn't mean she wants to feed us today."

"Women never get over their sweetheart days. Besides, I'll write her a check," Phil said. "She can name her price. She sells food for money all of the time. That's her profession. She'll feed us."

Duane hoped Phil was right. "She doesn't live at the café, though. Her place is five miles outside of town."

"Oh." Phil frowned. "I suppose that's too far to walk."

"Unless you want to faint from hunger on the way."

Phil was silent for a minute. "Didn't your great-aunt have anything at her house that runs? Some old car or anything?"

Duane thought a minute. "She had a small tractor in the barn that I used when I plowed up the garden plot every spring. That might still run."

"Well, let's go get it then." Phil stood up and started walking to the front of the bus. "What do you think Linda's making for Sunday dinner?"

"Meat loaf," Duane guessed. "She makes a wicked meat loaf."

Linda was a natural-born cook. He only hoped she was a natural-born hostess, as well. He didn't know many women who would appreciate two hungry men on their doorstep just as dinner was being pulled from the oven. He didn't dare bring up Phil's sweetheart theory, but he might use the café owner one.

Duane followed Phil out of the bus. He carefully put the sardine lid back on the tin as he walked by the counter. He didn't want the sardines to dry out just in case it turned out that the little fish were all he and Phil would have for Sunday dinner. They might be greeted at Linda's with the sound of a door slamming in their hungry faces.

Lucy saw the tractor coming down their driveway at the same time as Linda pulled the meat loaf out of the oven. Linda had already put the baked potatoes on a plate and the green peas in a bowl.

"I think it's the Jazz Man," Lucy called out. "And that friend of his."

"Phil?" Linda put the meat loaf on the top of the stove and walked to the window where Lucy was standing. "What are they doing out on that thing? Don't they know it's going to rain? They'll get soaked."

"They're just in time for dinner," Lucy said as she danced away from the window. "Isn't this great? Can I go invite them?"

Linda nodded. It was good to see Lucy so excited. "I'll put a couple more plates on the table."

Fortunately Linda always made a large Sunday

dinner because she and Lucy liked to have leftovers for a couple of days. There would be plenty of food for all four of them and she'd even brought a pie home with her last night from the café.

Linda heard the clatter of footsteps on the porch and Lucy's excited voice rising above the rumbles of the men. If she didn't know better, Linda would think she and her sister never had company for Sunday dinner given the amount of giggles she was hearing from Lucy.

Linda was just putting the meat loaf on the table when she realized why Lucy was so excited.

"Duane can sit in my place," Lucy said to the room at large. She'd already positioned the place mats closer together than usual. And they were the new red place mats, so they were hard to miss. "I'll sit on the other side by Phil."

Linda winced. Lucy was matchmaking.

"There's plenty of room at the table," Linda said. She had bought a round oak table at a secondhand store in Miles City. "Everyone can spread out if they want."

Linda figured Duane and Phil were too focused on the food to give Lucy's seating arrangement much thought. She moved her place mat a little as she sat down to eat. She hadn't moved it enough to make it offensive to the person sitting next to her. She just moved it enough to show no one needed to sit in the position Lucy had planned. They all had elbows, after all. They needed their space.

The silence was what tipped Duane off that something was happening. He'd sat down in the place Lucy had suggested and everyone else had found a place at the same time. But no one was passing the food or even talking.

Finally, Linda cleared her throat. "We usually say grace before eating."

"That's a fine tradition," Phil said with his eyes on the meat loaf.

"I know I'm thankful," Duane added as he sat up straighter in his chair. "You went to a lot of work."

Linda eyed him suspiciously. "You're supposed to be thankful to God for the food you eat."

Duane swallowed. "Okay. That, too."

Linda wasn't going to make it easy on him.

There was another minute of silence until Lucy nudged Linda and held out her hands to both Linda and Phil.

"We don't need to hold hands when we pray today," Linda said as she bowed her head.

"But we always do," Lucy protested. "Mama said that it brings everyone closer that way. The family that prays together stays together. Remember?"

"We're not a family," Linda muttered, but she did offer her hand to both Duane and Lucy.

"But we could have been a family," Lucy said. "If it hadn't been for me."

Lucy chose that moment to bow her head.

That left Duane looking over at Linda's stricken eyes. There was a pleading for help in those eyes that Duane couldn't ignore. So he did the only thing that came to mind.

"I'll pray," he offered as he grabbed hold of Linda's hand and bowed his own head. He had prayed before as a boy; he could do it again.

"Dear Father," Duane began. There that was easy. "I—I mean, we…ah…we thank you for the food." Duane thought there was something else he was supposed to add, but for the life of him he couldn't remember it. "That's all. Amen."

The other three people echoed his amen and lightning didn't strike him so Duane relaxed. Maybe God really was a forgiving sort.

Duane opened his eyes and he had something else to be thankful for—Linda was leaving her hand in his. Of course, that was probably only because she was keeping such a careful watch on Lucy's face that she wasn't paying any attention to her hand. Still, he hadn't held her hand for such a long time and it was a moment to relish even if Phil was sitting there looking at everyone as though he was gathering something juicy for the tabloids.

"Nothing's your fault, Lucy," Duane said. "Your sister loves you. That's all."

"But she loved you, too," Lucy said with a sigh as she turned her face to Duane. "I never meant to come between two people so truly in love they wanted to be married."

Lucy sighed again and looked like the fifteen-year-old she was.

"True love?" Phil asked with a quick look from Duane to Linda. "I knew you were sweethearts, but I didn't know you two were going to—"

Linda shook her head. "I never told you that, Lucy. Besides, it's all in the past."

"It was my fault," Duane admitted. He'd thought about having this conversation with Linda many times, but he'd never pictured an audience like this one. Still, a man had to take what chances he had. "I was a young kid and I thought there was always tomorrow and besides with my early years—"

Linda shook her head. "It was *nobody's* fault. It's just the way it was. Now, who wants some meat loaf?"

Duane had eaten his first bite of meat loaf before it hit him. It didn't matter whose fault it was or how many explanations he gave for his behavior. He still had thrown away his chance to sit down at this table for the past eight years instead of bouncing around on the road in that bus. Linda had made a home here; he could have been part of that home. This could have been his life.

"I like what you've done with the place." Duane looked around. The table was in the middle of the old-fashioned kitchen and the counters were tiled in a black-and-white pattern that reminded him of the café.

Now this was what a kitchen should be. It was obvious someone actually cooked in it unlike the designer kitchen in his house in Hollywood. The only appliances he knew were in working order there were the refrigerator and the microwave. That's because he kept his water bottles cold in the refrigerator and made his coffee in the microwave. He had some fancy gourmet stove with convection ovens and a built-in griddle. But he never used any of them. He was gone so much that he didn't even keep food in the house.

Suddenly, all of the adventures he'd planned to have when he left Dry Creek years ago didn't seem so appealing. There were times when he wondered if he hadn't been running away from his dreams instead of toward them that day he left.

"Linda made the curtains herself," Lucy said proudly as she laid her fork on her plate. "And we both painted the inside of the house."

"It's nice." The curtains were white with a red band and the walls were white, as well. Bright red jars lined the counter and green plants stood on the windowsill. "Very nice."

"Lance painted the outside of the house for us," Lucy said.

Duane frowned at that. He supposed he couldn't object to Lance helping Linda, but he didn't have to like it. He wasn't quite sure why, but it just didn't sit right with him. This was supposed to have been his life, not Lance's.

Linda looked up at him. "I suppose I owe you some for the house, too. I took a loan against the café for a down payment and since the café was half yours, even if it wasn't on paper that way, then—"

Duane shook his head. "Whatever you think you owe me, I'm canceling it all when you sing with me."

"For the press conference?" Phil asked. "She's singing with you?"

"Sorry. I forgot to tell you," Duane muttered.

"Don't worry about it," Phil said with a slow smile. "That's good news. The more the merrier."

"I don't want her mentioned in the press, though." Duane scowled at Phil. He wouldn't wish the press on anyone and certainly not on Linda. "Just say she's a local woman I hired to sing with me."

"Well, that's the truth. That's all I am," Linda said brightly as she pushed her chair back from the table and stood up. "Now, does anyone want dessert?"

Duane swore he was as clumsy with things now as he had been when he left Dry Creek. "You know that's not all you are. It's just that we can't tell the truth to the reporters."

"You should always tell the truth," Lucy said. "Mama said the truth will set you free."

"That was the Bible, Luce," Linda said as she walked to the table with the blackberry pie in her hands. "Mama didn't say that. Of course, you should tell the truth anyway."

Lucy nodded in agreement.

Duane tried to catch Linda's eye.

"Of course," Linda continued as she set the pie on the table, "that doesn't mean you need to *volunteer* information to people when it's none of their business."

Duane relaxed. "Like the reporters."

Linda nodded. "Yes, like the reporters. If they ask questions, you can always say you have no comment."

"Oh," Lucy said.

"Especially if they ask personal questions about other people," Linda added.

"You can always ask them to talk to me if they're giving you a hard time," Phil offered. "I know how to keep a secret."

"Nothing's a secret," Linda said. "It's just private. There's a difference."

"They might not ask any questions anyway," Duane added. "Phil will have a press release for them. That'll tell them the basics."

"Well, they will want some local color," Phil protested. "We'll have to give them that."

Duane nodded. "I suppose so, but that doesn't mean they need to pry into my personal life with Linda."

Linda's head snapped up at that. "You have no personal life with me."

"Well, maybe not now, but—" Duane felt a headache coming on.

"If the reporters want to know about Duane's early life, they can go visit his old house," Linda said. "It's just the way it was when his great-aunt died."

"She'd have a fit if I let people into the place like it is now," Duane said. Mrs. Hargrove had given him a key and he'd visited the house yesterday. "There's dust everywhere. My great-aunt was a proud housekeeper."

"The youth group at church is talking about doing a car wash," Lucy said. "Maybe you could pay us to clean your house after school someday."

"It would certainly make it look better," Phil said.

"We don't charge too much," Lucy added.

"I don't care what it costs, I'll pay top dollar."

"Really?" Lucy brightened. "We're raising money to take a trip to a youth conference in Seattle. We were going to charge five dollars an hour for odd jobs."

"I'll make it twenty-five," Duane said.

"Really? For everybody?"

Duane nodded. "Everybody who shows up and works."

Linda shrugged. "Sounds pretty generous to me. But it's a good solution. You won't have enough time to get everything done if you try to do it yourself. When are the reporters coming anyway?"

"Friday," Phil said. "They wanted to be able to get their bearings before the church service on Sunday."

"That gives you four days," Linda said.

"We can be there at three-thirty tomorrow to clean," Lucy said. "We'll start right after school."

"Sounds good to me." Duane wondered if he'd finally feel as though he'd come home when his old home was swept and dusted.

"Don't get rid of any of the charm, though," Phil cautioned. "You know, old calendars, old toys—that kind of thing…"

"I never had toys."

"I suppose we could put your old guitar in the house," Linda said. "That was the closest thing you had to a toy."

"No, the guitar stays in the café," Duane said. "That's where it belongs."

"Nobody there knows how to play it," Linda said.

"Still, that's where it belongs."

It had always given Duane a good feeling to know that his guitar was with Linda. That guitar was all he had left of his life in Chicago and it seemed as though it belonged here, with Linda. He liked knowing she had it. And that she was able to look in on Boots from time to time. Mrs. Hargrove had told him that Linda often had a bone for Boots. And that Linda sat and talked with Lance when he was missing life on the reservation.

It wasn't until he put it all together that Duane realized he'd left his life in Linda's hands when he left. And she'd taken care of it for him. Looking back, he wondered why she'd done it. He'd always thought she'd be better off without him in her life, but maybe he had been wrong. Maybe she'd cared more about him than he would have believed possible.

Maybe he'd given up more when he left Dry Creek

than he'd ever dreamed he could have in this life. He should have taken a chance that he'd figure out how to be part of a family before Linda figured out he was no good at it. After all, he always wanted what was best for her. Maybe that would have been enough. Which reminded him…

"We're planning to pay for dinner today," Duane said. "I forgot to mention it earlier. Just add it to our next café bill."

Linda's shoulders stiffened. "I don't sell food on Sundays."

"Well, but we tracked you down and barged in here."

"You're both invited guests."

"Well, then, thank you." Duane's voice wavered.

"You're welcome."

Linda didn't look any too pleased with him when she said any of the polite words. He'd probably said everything backward to her. Duane wondered if he would ever figure out how to blend in with others. His great-aunt Cornelia had tried to show him how other people lived, but he'd learned his lessons early on the streets of Chicago. No one there would turn down money if someone offered it to them in exchange for Sunday dinner. Even the soup kitchens had a donation bucket at the end of the line.

Chapter Eight

"Did you bring the ketchup?" Lucy danced around as Linda walked up the steps to the Enger house and Lucy jumped down the same steps to greet her. "The kids are loving this! We've never had someone give us hamburgers before we even started a job!"

It was late afternoon and the sky was overcast. The two-story frame house had been lit up as Linda pulled her small wheeled cart down the driveway. She had left Phil back at the café making some phone calls. She'd left a note on the door telling any customers that she'd be back in thirty minutes. Not that anyone would come in. Most people in Dry Creek were at the Enger house already. Even a lot of the nearby ranch people were there.

The ones who drove into Dry Creek had parked their cars at the beginning of the drive and walked the rest of the way to the house because the bus was still stuck right in the middle of the lane. The utility workers had evidently gotten through somehow because every window in the house shone with artificial light.

Linda let Lucy enter the kitchen first and then let the screen door close behind them. The faint smell of disinfectant told her some of the kitchen had already been cleaned. It probably hadn't been done by the kids, though, because she could hear the orientation speech still taking place in the living room of the house. She could even see what was happening through the doorway. Dust covers had been pulled off the furniture and every teenager held a mop or a broom or a brush of some sort.

Linda set the box of hamburgers down on the scrubbed kitchen counter and turned to her sister. "Yes, I've got the ketchup and the mustard. I've packed lots of hamburgers to go, you know."

"The Jazz Man has us divided into teams," Lucy said as she helped Linda pull the condiment packets out of a separate bag. "Isn't he just the best?"

Linda grunted. "I hope he knows we don't ordinarily do deliveries. Takeouts, yes. Deliveries, no."

Linda handed Lucy a plastic platter from the side of the box.

It sounded like all of the teenagers in Dry Creek, and most of their grandparents, were lined up to work so Linda knew she better get the food out. Through the doorway she saw Mrs. Hargrove tying an apron on one of the girls. Not only had Duane promised every worker twenty-five dollars an hour for cleaning, he'd also suggested an overall two-hundred-dollar bonus toward their trip fund when everyone finished the job. And if that wasn't wonderful enough, then he had ordered them all hamburgers for an afternoon snack before they even started.

The prayer chain had gone wild, asking everyone who could hold a broom to come and help with the cleaning. Linda wondered if Duane knew what he had done. There hadn't been this much excitement around since the pastor's twins thought they'd found gold nuggets in the bottom of the Big Dry Creek.

Linda knew she should relax. The man was trying to do a good thing for the kids in Dry Creek and she couldn't fault him for that. They'd make more money cleaning this house than they would in the rest of their fund-raising time, especially with all of the adults who were volunteering to help them with the work. They might raise enough for the conference fees from today alone.

It's just that it wasn't real.

Each of those adults in the living room had more commitment to the youth of Dry Creek than Duane Enger did. And yet he got to be the hero. No one paid that kind of money around here for simple cleaning. And the bonus was pure giveaway money. He was practically paying people to think he was somebody great. Linda wondered if he'd be doing something like this if those reporters weren't coming to town later this week. It was so transparent to her; she didn't understand why no one else seemed aware of what was motivating Duane.

"He's really a good person," Lucy said as she stopped arranging hamburgers wrapped in foil on the platter and glanced up at Linda. "I didn't know him much before, but he's all right. Really. The kids all think so."

Linda looked over at her sister. "I hope they're basing that opinion on more than the fact that he's giving all of you free hamburgers."

Lucy wrinkled her nose and grinned. "He also pays really good."

"Oh, well, that makes it better."

Linda saw Mrs. Hargrove walking toward the doorway. The older woman was probably coming to see if the hamburgers were ready to be served.

"Seriously," Lucy said as she handed the platter to Linda. "I think you and he could—you know—have a future."

Linda almost dropped the platter. She turned and set the platter down before putting her arm around her sister. "Lucy, he's not staying here. He's putting on a press conference, that's all. This is all—" Linda waved her arm around the kitchen, including Mrs. Hargrove, who now stood in the doorway "—designed to make him look good so people will say good things about him to the reporters so everyone will buy his CD."

Lucy looked up at her and Linda saw all of the confused hope in her younger sister's eyes. "But the love you guys had for each other, that's still there, right? Love doesn't just *die*."

"Him being here—it's just business." Linda hugged her sister. "But that doesn't mean you shouldn't have a good time. Go find out if they have enough sodas out front."

Lucy nodded as she walked away.

Linda looked up at Mrs. Hargrove. "The hamburgers are almost ready. Let me just get the rest of them on a platter."

Mrs. Hargrove nodded as she stepped closer to the counter where Linda was stacking wrapped hamburgers on a large platter.

"Lucy will be fine," Mrs. Hargrove said. "You don't need to worry so much about her."

Linda nodded and blinked away the moisture in her eyes. She'd made fifty hamburgers and she was suddenly wondering if that would be enough.

"How are *you?*" Mrs. Hargrove asked as she stepped even closer.

"Oh, me, I'm fine." Linda blinked again. "Business is good and—"

Mrs. Hargrove just opened her arms and Linda walked right into them.

"What's wrong with me?" Linda tried to stop the tears, but she couldn't seem to. "It's been eight years. I should be fine. I should be so totally over him. He's a jerk anyway."

Mrs. Hargrove just held her and patted her back. "It's okay to be upset. I sometimes think you work as hard convincing Lucy that everything in life is perfect as you do in telling yourself that nothing is going to work out for you. You're the pessimist so Lucy can be the optimist."

"Lucy's my little sister. I don't want her to think—"

"I know." Mrs. Hargrove gave Linda's shoulders a squeeze. "But we can't shelter anyone from all of life's unpleasantness no matter how much we love them."

"I just want her to be happy. And to think people love her."

"I know, dear. I know." Mrs. Hargrove gave Linda a final pat on the shoulder. "But how can anyone really know God's love if they never have any problems in their life? And, you. What makes you always so certain that the fairy tales you spin for Lucy could never be true for you?"

Linda stepped away. "Someone's got to have a head on their shoulders."

Mrs. Hargrove smiled a little sadly. "I should have paid more attention to the two of you girls even before your mother died. You shouldn't have to worry about making things rosier for Lucy than they really are. Telling her all those things your mother said."

"You know?" Linda looked at the older woman. "I haven't been lying to her exactly. I just wanted her to think she was special to our mother."

"I know."

"Our mother, she didn't—"

"I know," Mrs. Hargrove said. "That's why I wish I had paid more attention. So you would both have known that you were loved. And lovable. Like with Duane…"

Linda stepped back as if she'd been stung. "This has nothing to do with Duane. He doesn't love anyone around here. If his great-aunt hadn't died, he would have left her behind, too. He didn't even keep Boots with him, remember? He couldn't be bothered."

"Is that what you think?" Mrs. Hargrove stood still. "Oh, dear, that's not how it was at all. He brought Boots to me because the poor dog was miserable in Hollywood. With all the noise. And no place to run. Duane tried a kennel when he was on tour, but that was even worse. He sent Boots here for the dog's own good."

Linda started stacking hamburgers on the platter again. "You're too kind to Duane. I bet he's even stopped paying you for the dog biscuits Boots eats."

"Oh." Mrs. Hargrove drew in a breath. "He pays me

for more than the dog biscuits, dear. He's been paying my property taxes all these years. And my water bill. I wouldn't be able to afford to stay in my house anymore if he wasn't paying those taxes for me. And, that's in addition to the dog biscuits and Boots's vet bills and—"

Linda looked up. "I'm sorry. I didn't know. I just thought—"

"Don't underestimate Duane Enger." Mrs. Hargrove smiled. "He's got a heart of gold. He just doesn't want everyone to know it. He was devoted to Cornelia, too, in his own way."

A cheer went up in the living room.

Mrs. Hargrove nodded toward the sound. "He'll make someone a fine husband. Now that he's back, I have such high hopes."

Linda didn't know what to say to the older woman so she just finished stacking the hamburgers on the platter until Lucy came back and said everyone was ready to eat.

Duane sat on the staircase in his great-aunt's living room and watched everyone eating their hamburgers. He hadn't had such a good time in years. Not many kids could make a party out of a housecleaning. He was impressed, too, that so many adults had come to help out. The retired men he'd met the other morning at Linda's café were all there. And some middle-aged women who appeared to be mothers. Dry Creek cared about their teenagers; that was for sure.

Duane had been eating his own hamburger so he didn't pay any attention to the silence at first. Then, just as he finished the best hamburger he'd ever eaten, he heard the sound of boots in the kitchen and saw several of the hands from the Elkton Ranch walk into the living room.

To a man, they all removed their Stetson hats. They wore faded jeans and Western shirts. These were the men Duane had seen in church on Sunday.

"We heard the kids needed help," Lance said. He seemed to be the spokesperson for the group. "So we came to help."

"Mopping?" Duane asked, a smile curling his lips. He'd pay extra to see Lance Walker mop a floor.

Lance's face was stiff with determination. "We plan to do our part. That's what being part of the body of Christ is about. Helping out our fellow believers."

Duane wiped his hands as he stood up. "Well, there's plenty of work for everyone. And Mrs. Hargrove has enough aprons to go around."

Just then Mrs. Hargrove came into the living room from the kitchen shaking her head. "You know those boys aren't going to wear my aprons."

"Yes, ma'am," Duane said with a grin. "I suppose that's true."

"We thought we might be able to clean out the barn," Lance said and he seemed to relax a little.

"That barn hasn't had any animals in it for twenty years," Duane protested. His great-aunt Cornelia kept threatening to buy a milk cow after Duane got there, but she never did. "All of the dirt was blown out of there decades ago."

"We brought a few old boards in case we needed to do some patching instead. We figured it might be a little drafty in there."

"Then, the barn it is," Duane agreed. He rather liked seeing Lance all purposeful like this. And surrounded by his friends.

Duane had debated for hours last night about whether or not Lance was serious when he gave his talk in church. Oh, he knew Lance believed what he was saying. Lance always was a straight shooter. He just didn't know if Lance had given any consideration to the implications of what he was saying.

A man giving his life to God was a big move. It was like signing an exclusive contract for the next fifty years with a company and not even seeing their business plan. Duane wouldn't mind talking to Lance about his decision some, just to be sure his old friend knew what he was doing. Just as a gesture of friendship and concern.

Duane had walked halfway across the living room to mention this to Lance when Linda stepped out of the kitchen, carrying another platter of hamburgers.

Linda, of course, stopped right in front of Lance and the other ranch hands and offered them the hamburgers.

Lance took one and flashed a smile at Linda. "Thanks, sweetheart."

Duane stopped walking. He didn't even listen to what the other ranch hands had to say when they took their hamburgers off the platter. He knew it was true that Linda might date one of these men, but none of them were going to call her sweetheart. Not in his house. Not when he was paying them a prime wage. That's what he used to call Linda.

"Let's take a look at the barn now," Duane said as he looked directly at Lance. "You and me."

"I haven't finished my hamburger."

"Bring it with you," Duane said as he finished walking through the living room. He heard Lance's footsteps as he followed.

The air outside the house was chilly and it had drizzled a little in the last few minutes.

Duane stopped on the back porch and took a deep breath before he turned to the other man. "I hope you're not too religious to meet me behind the barn."

Lance gave a slow smile as he wrapped what was left of his hamburger more securely in its paper and placed it on the step railing. "As I recall, you owe me one."

"I didn't fight you before, because I didn't know what in the world you were mad about." Duane stomped off the porch and headed to the barn.

"And you figure you know all about it now?" Lance followed him.

"I figure I know enough." Duane rolled up the sleeves on his shirt as he kept walking.

"You best take that apron off, too."

"I don't have any apron on and you know it." Duane couldn't help but look down to check. Those girls had been going around tying aprons on everyone. "And even if I did have one on, it wouldn't matter. I can take you anytime, anyplace, apron or not."

"Yeah, and who's going to help you do that?"

Duane had remembered the ground behind his great-aunt's barn as being soft with grass. Over the years, the grass had all died. There was nothing but hard dirt.

Duane and Lance stood looking at each other. They had sized each other up in this same spot a dozen times while they were in high school.

"I suppose you're worried about your face," Lance said as he looked at Duane. "Now that you're famous."

"I'm not worried about anything."

"Me, neither."

Duane figured Lance should make the first move. "What's wrong? Don't Christians fight? Don't tell me you've turned into a sissy?"

Lance moved first, but their fists both landed about the same time.

The sound of their knuckles hitting flesh was followed by the stern voice of Mrs. Hargrove. "What do you boys think you're doing?"

It was the voice that had stopped mischief for generations in Dry Creek.

"Ah," Duane said as he moved a little away from Lance and steadied them both. "We're…ah…"

"We were having a theological discussion." Lance finally found his footing. "On…ah…what it means to be a Christian."

"I wasn't born yesterday," Mrs. Hargrove snapped back. She had her hands on her hips and her apron securely tied over her gingham housedress.

"It was my fault," Duane confessed. "I brought him out here."

"But I came willingly."

"There's got to be a better way to settle your problems," Mrs. Hargrove said. Her voice lost some of its steel. "Have you tried praying about them?"

"No, ma'am, I can't say we have." Lance looked over at Duane. "I don't even know for sure what the problem here is."

Duane snorted in disbelief. "You knew very well I'd object to you calling Linda your sweetheart."

A slow grin spread across Lance's face. "You objected to that now, did you?"

"Well, no harm was done," Mrs. Hargrove said with a smile of her own as she turned to go back. "Don't be long now. Everyone is waiting to get started."

Duane saw the bruise starting to form on Lance's face, just above his left cheekbone.

"I shouldn't have said that about you becoming a sissy now that you're a Christian," Duane apologized. "I don't think you could be a coward no matter what you became."

"That's all right. I can always say now that I've been persecuted for my faith." Lance grinned.

"I haven't been persecuting you and you know it. I'm trying to be nice and say I think it's okay. You and this Christian stuff."

"Really?"

Duane nodded. "Just don't hug me again, okay?"

Lance grinned. "So it really made you mad when I called Linda my sweetheart, huh?"

"Does that mean you've been dating her?" Duane tried not to look at Lance when he asked this question.

"I've been asking her to go out with me for over a year now."

Duane looked up. "Oh."

Lance grinned. "Of course, she hasn't said yes yet. But I figure I'm wearing her down."

Duane nodded. He felt better already.

"She's not going out with anyone else, either," Lance offered. "But she's not going to stay single forever."

Duane was already walking back to the house. He didn't need an up-to-date account of Linda's dating life. He didn't know why he should make such a big deal, either. It was probably because none of the men around here were good enough for her. He just wanted to see her hooked up with someone worthy, that was all. Linda deserved the best.

Chapter Nine

Duane could feel the soreness around his eye before he woke up. He had moved back into his childhood bedroom after everyone left yesterday. Phil had slept in the guest room and the morning light which was now coming into Duane's window had probably woken Phil up by now, as well.

Duane had hoped the ice pack he'd put on the eye last night would have made the swelling go down enough that it wouldn't be so bad this morning. He got out of bed and walked to the mirror in his room before he admitted to himself a night's sleep had not helped very much. The whole area around his left eye was a shining black-and-blue bruise. He looked as if he'd collided with a football player or, maybe even, a semitrailer. He doubted anyone yesterday had believed him when he'd said he'd missed a ball Lance had thrown toward him, but no one had challenged his story.

Except Phil. The manager had finished his calls in the café and had come back to Duane's house just before Duane and Lance entered the kitchen.

Phil had taken one look at Duane and pulled him back out on the porch. Then he had demanded to know what Duane was thinking.

"We've got the press coming," Phil had hissed in Duane's ear. "You better have a good story to go with that shiner."

Duane checked to see that the kitchen door was firmly closed. He couldn't guarantee that people were not listening at the windows, though. He'd already noticed some cameras among the teenagers. Hopefully they still wouldn't want a picture of him. He didn't look much like his fan photo at the moment.

"I had a disagreement," Duane mumbled with his head down. "That's all."

Duane didn't want the whole town of Dry Creek to be gossiping about him and Linda. He knew Mrs. Hargrove would mind her own business and Lance wasn't likely to tell what had happened. But Duane couldn't vouch for everyone inside the house.

"Not good enough," Phil said. He glanced at the windows, too, and lowered his voice. "The press won't be content with a story like that. Your fans won't, either. They want to respect you."

"Since when?"

Duane knew he shouldn't be giving Phil a hard time. The man was just trying to do his job. But it suddenly seemed more than Duane could bear. "Since when do they need to respect me? I'm singing them a song in church on Sunday. That's all I agreed to do. That has to be enough."

Phil stepped closer to Duane. "Well, just answer me this. What is so important that you need to fight about it when you haven't even been back in this town for eight long years?"

"Nothing."

Or everything, Duane thought to himself. "I just want the best for—" Duane ducked his head so no one could even read his lips. "For Linda—she deserves a better husband than Lance."

"So what's wrong with this guy? Is he an alcoholic?"

Duane shook his head.

"Likely to run around on her?"

Duane shook his head. Lance was true-blue. Everyone knew that.

"Lazy? So she'd have to do all the work?"

"No, he's a good worker."

Phil scowled. "So what's wrong with the man that justifies you messing up a press conference?"

Duane shrugged. "Nothing, I guess. But that doesn't mean I can't have an opinion."

"What you've got isn't an opinion." Phil stomped off the porch and turned to look over his shoulder. "What you've got is unresolved issues."

Duane watched his manager march back down the lane toward the bus. He couldn't remember when Phil had ever gotten so genuinely upset. Fortunately he hadn't mentioned any names when his voice got louder.

The sound of the kitchen door opening made Duane turn around.

Linda came outside. She had a small tube in her hand. "It's really for burns, but it was all anyone had."

"You asked everyone?" Duane protested.

Linda took the lid off the tube. "It's hardly a secret

that you and Lance went out behind the barn and took a swing at each other."

"Oh."

Linda gestured toward the first step. "Go ahead and sit down and I'll put some of this on for you."

"I suppose Lance is in there telling everyone about it." Duane sat on the step.

"You know better than that." Linda spread some ointment around Duane's eye.

Duane held his breath. Suddenly, he didn't care what anyone was saying about him. Linda was so close he could see the pulse in her throat. Her hands moved around his eye with a gentleness he had no right to expect. She wore a thin white blouse with a pointed collar. The collar moved with her arms as she reached over to soothe his eye. He put his arm up to steady her as she leaned over him. Seeing her like this brought back a flood of memories.

"Kiss me," Duane whispered.

He felt the surprise run through her. He was a little startled himself.

"Why?" she asked quietly as she leaned back a little.

Duane moved himself up to a higher step so he was level with her. He might not have planned this, but he wanted it more than he wanted some ointment. "Because. Just because."

Duane could read the indecision in her eyes. She had such beautiful eyes.

"Please," he added.

He saw her eyes soften. That was all the invitation he needed. He leaned into her lips and kissed her fully. She sighed and leaned a little closer to him. He put both arms around her and pulled her as close as she could come. He felt he'd finally come home. He had Linda in his arms.

And then there was a flash. And another one.

Then Mrs. Hargrove was raising her voice. "Put away your cameras and get away from the windows, everyone. People are entitled to some privacy."

And then there was another flash. This one came from the path leading up to the steps. Phil had returned with his camera.

Linda looked from Duane to Phil and back again. "So, this was for a picture."

"No," Duane said, but Linda was already backing away. There was no softness in her eyes now.

"I hope you got what you needed for your press conference," Linda said as she stood up.

"This has nothing to do with the press conference," Duane protested, turning to Phil. "Tell her. What do you have your camera for anyway?"

Phil shrugged. "I was going to take a picture of the kids working inside. That was what I brought the camera for. That was going to be for the press conference."

"See," Duane said as he turned to Linda. "The kiss has nothing to do with the press conference."

Linda turned. She already was opening the kitchen door. "The kiss had nothing to do with anything."

With that, Linda stepped inside the kitchen.

Duane had followed her back inside, but it was pointless. Linda hadn't been able to look him in the eye for the rest of the time she was at his house. She left as soon as the kids had finished most of the hamburgers. She loaded the used papers in her empty boxes and put the leftover hamburgers in the refrigerator. Then she pulled her little cart back to the café. Duane just watched her leave.

The rest of the day had been subdued. The old men did some dusting, but they kept scowling at Duane. The teenagers washed floors and then looked at Duane as though he'd sprouted a third eye in the middle of his forehead. Every time he went into a room all of the workers' chatter stopped. Duane supposed he had messed things up pretty bad for a man who was supposed to be a star of some kind.

The only one who didn't avoid Duane was Lance. His old friend even came to him and asked if Duane wanted him and the other ranch hands to hose off the porch. The answer was yes.

Duane was relieved when it came time to write a check and tell everyone goodbye so he could head to his old room in peace. He had barely told Phil where to bunk down for the night before Duane himself lay down on his childhood bed and went to sleep.

There had been the hope in Duane's mind just before he went to sleep that everything would be fine the next morning. He told himself the ointment Linda had put on his eye would work wonders. Maybe the bruise wouldn't be so noticeable. And maybe Linda would have decided she liked the kiss he gave her.

The next morning, he didn't have to look farther than the bruise on his face to know nothing had improved during the night.

"What do you plan to do?" Phil asked as Duane walked down the steps.

Phil was sitting at the dining room table with a cold hamburger on his plate. Everything in the dining room shone with cleanliness and smelled of lemon. The windows were spotless. All of Great-Aunt Cornelia's china sparkled in the cabinet.

"I plan to go forward just like we've talked about doing," Duane said. "There's no reason I can't sing. I'll think of something to tell the press if they ask about my bruise."

"Oh, they'll ask. And don't try the ball in the face story," Phil said. "That one doesn't sound sincere. It's like the dog who ate my homework. Even if it were true, nobody would believe it."

"So, maybe I fell. The press isn't coming here to look at my face anyway. They want to listen to me sing in church."

"They're coming to measure you in every way." Phil picked up the cold hamburger. "Make no mistake about it. They'll want to know everything."

"Well." Duane sat down at the table. "They're not going to know everything. I don't want Linda's name mentioned in that press conference."

Phil took a bite of his hamburger and chewed it slowly. "I won't mention her unless I absolutely need to."

Duane finally understood why Phil was eating that cold hamburger. Phil had his own code of ethics. He wouldn't be eating at the café any more because he knew he might sell Linda down the river.

Both men were silent for a moment.

"I'm forbidding you to mention Linda," Duane finally said. "You're the manager, I have the final say."

"The band has the final say," Phil corrected him as he put the remainder of his hamburger back on his plate. "And I've already called and gotten their permission to do what I need to do."

Duane forced himself to take a breath. Then he let it out. He knew with stone-cold certainty. "You do it and I'll quit the band."

Phil snorted. "And leave the kind of gig you all have? I don't think so. The guys are picking up hordes of new fans south of the border already. I talked to them. We'll be set."

"Then call off the whole press conference."

Phil shook his head. "That would raise more questions than it would answer. No, we'll go through with it and we'll just hope for the best. Maybe they'll be content with your song and a few words from you."

Duane guessed he would have to work on his song today. At least his voice was doing better. And Linda had promised to meet him at the church at eleven o'clock to begin practicing. If he had a magnificent song and a few words that sounded sincere, maybe the press would be satisfied and go home.

All he really wanted was for everyone to leave him alone so he could think about what it meant that Linda had returned his kiss. At least he thought she'd returned it. Maybe it had just been the surprise of it all.

Of course, it would make no difference if she was feeling friendlier toward him. Not if the press decided to use her in their stories. Well, he just needed to make sure the reporters didn't know about her. Which meant the first thing he needed to do today was to pick out an impressive song, something that would keep everyone's attention on music.

Linda stood at the counter in the café polishing a coffee cup. There was no reason in the world to be standing there rubbing that thing with a corner of her apron, but she found herself doing it without even realizing she was.

Something was wrong with her.

She'd teared up and cried this morning for no reason, too. Right after Charley gave his order for eggs over easy, she'd choked up and had to excuse herself. When she came back, Charley said he'd settle for coffee and toast. Elmer hadn't even ordered anything; he said he'd be happy to bring the coffeepot out of the kitchen for her and serve anyone who wanted any. He'd even brought out the cream.

Linda had sat down and told her grandfathers that she was okay and that they didn't need to worry about her.

"It's really for the best," she found herself saying to them. "Duane will be gone before anyone knows it and then I can move on and date someone else."

Charley grunted. "What if he doesn't go?"

Linda looked at Charley. "Well, of course he's going." Linda stopped. She hadn't realized all that meant until now. "Poor Boots. He'll start to miss him all over again. It's just not fair."

Linda had to stop and blink for a second or two. "That poor dog."

There was a minute of silence.

Finally, Elmer cleared his throat. "I wonder what

would happen if that press conference went bad. Maybe then Duane would be content to stay in Dry Creek."

Linda breathed in. "We can't—"

Charley shook his head. "No, it wouldn't be right."

Elmer shrugged. "I'm just saying what if. No harm in thinking what might happen. There's a lot that can go wrong with those reporters around."

"I won't have anyone doing anything to harm Duane," Linda said softly. "Even if it is for Boots. That dog will just have to find another master to worry over."

Charley reached over and put his hand over Linda's hand that was lying on the table. "We'll be here for you. Don't you fret."

"Oh, I'm not worried," Linda said brightly as she stood up. "I should go get Boots a big bone out of the freezer. I'll thaw it out and give it to him later today. That might make him feel better."

Linda walked back to the kitchen.

The door to the café opened when Linda was in the kitchen unwrapping the bone for Boots. She wondered if it was Mrs. Hargrove.

Linda walked out of the kitchen, wiping her hands on a dish towel.

There stood Duane.

Duane could tell he wasn't welcome. The old men sitting at the table closest to the kitchen looked at him as though he were interrupting something. The furnace was putting out a steady heat, however, and the air felt good after his walk over from the house.

"I was hoping I could buy a pot of coffee," Duane said. He didn't know why he was taking pity on Phil, but he'd left the manager back at the house trying to eat his second cold hamburger and Duane's heart had softened. There was no reason to add caffeine withdrawal to their problems.

"And maybe some hot biscuits and hard-boiled eggs," Duane said and forced himself to smile. The biscuits and eggs were things that carried easily. "And any bananas that you might have. Or apples."

Linda nodded and stepped back into the kitchen.

Duane held back his sigh. He had no right to expect that Linda would have thought about what happened yesterday afternoon and decided that the kiss they had shared meant something to her. Still, he had hoped she might return his smile just a little.

"I'll be going soon," Duane said as he looked at the old men at the table. None of them were smiling at him, either. "I just want to warm up before I head back to the house."

There was a moment's silence. Duane checked to see that his guitar still hung on the wall of the café. Someone had hung the framed letter back up, as well. At least that made him feel good. He knew he'd remember that guitar hanging there when he was on the road again.

It was so quiet Duane could hear Linda moving around back in the kitchen.

"The springtimes aren't always this cold around here," Elmer finally said. "A young fellow like you would do well with our weather."

Duane looked at the man. "You have fierce winters. Snowstorms."

"But it's bracing," Charley said. "It's good for a man to have these cold winters. Keeps your blood healthy."

Duane grunted and nodded to the men. He wasn't going to argue with them about what kept people healthy. The old men were just passing the time of day anyway. He might be surprised they were passing it with him, but he wasn't going to argue with them.

It was silent for another minute and Duane wondered what was keeping Linda. Maybe he should have just asked for raw eggs. He could cook the biscuits at his place, too, now that the utilities were turned on.

"So, have you given any thought to staying?" Elmer finally asked.

"What?" Duane said as Linda stepped out of the kitchen, carrying a white bag and a large thermos jug.

"Oh," Elmer said as he looked down at the floor.

"We're just worried about Boots," Charley said as he looked at his feet, as well.

"What's wrong with Boots?" Duane looked over at the men. Did they know something he didn't know? "Has someone noticed something about Boots?"

"They're just worried about how your dog will react when you leave," Linda said as she handed the bag to Duane with a fierce look. "It isn't right to get him attached to you again when you're just going to go back to your Hollywood show dog in a week."

Duane looked at her. "I don't have another dog."

"Oh, well, still," Linda said as she held the thermos out to Duane. "Please return the thermos, if you can manage."

"I can manage." Duane didn't like the assumption that he was a careless person who didn't return things or take care of his dog. "Maybe I need to talk to Mrs. Hargrove about getting a different kind of dog food for Boots."

"That woman is a saint," Charley said abruptly. "She cooks for that dog! There isn't anything wrong with the food Boots gets."

"I never meant there was." Duane walked toward the door. He couldn't win with this group. "Boots probably eats better than I do."

Especially now, Duane thought as he held the thermos a little closer.

Charley grunted.

Duane waited until he had the door opened before he turned around and called to Linda. "I'll see you at eleven at the church."

He closed the door before anyone could answer him. He didn't want to give anyone a chance to interfere with the schedule for today. He and Linda needed to practice if they were going to pull off a worthwhile show for the reporters.

He just had time to carry the coffee and food back to the house before he needed to head for the church. Hopefully, no one here objected to him practicing in the church. If Duane lived to be a hundred, he didn't think he'd ever understand the people of Dry Creek. He was almost convinced that Elmer had actually invited him to stay in the town. But that didn't make any sense. He'd never gotten along with those old men.

Chapter Ten

Linda was punctual. She walked up the steps to the church at five minutes to eleven. She decided God was giving her a chance to show how much He meant to her. If she could help Duane sing a song of praise to God in front of all those reporters, surely God would be pleased with her. Even if Duane didn't mean what he was singing, she would mean it and maybe people could see how much she believed in God.

It would be her gift to God. And she wouldn't complain. After all, there was a time when believers were burned at the stake for their faith. All she had to do was stand up beside a hypocrite and let her faith shine.

She wouldn't even let Duane discourage her, she told herself as she opened the doors and stepped into the foyer of the church.

She only hesitated a moment when she saw Duane talking to Pastor Curtis at the front of the church.

Duane turned and saw Linda coming into the church. She stood at the back, looking uncertain of what to do.

Duane had already told the pastor that he was in need
of a magnificent song even if he didn't have the feelings
to be truthfully singing it. Duane wanted to be as forth-
right as he could be about what he was going to do.

"I don't know." Pastor Curtis was frowning a little.
"I would recommend matching your beliefs to the song
more closely."

Duane shook his head. "I'm faking it most of the time
when I sing with the band anyway. It doesn't need to be
real."

"You know," the pastor said slowly, "it's been my observation that God will meet you where you are if you're
honest with Him. A sincere song of doubt would work.
I'm not sure there's any need to fake a song."

"Oh, there's a need," Duane said as he watched Linda
walk toward them. "I don't have time to worry about
God. I need something impressive by Sunday."

"There's a song of doubt that's in Latin," the pastor
said. "I could recommend that."

"Latin?" Duane watched as Linda walked up to him.
"Now that might work."

"It does have lots of hallelujahs in it for the end," the
pastor added. "It only begins with the songwriter's
doubts. But you could sing most of it with meaning."

"I think we've got our song," Duane said to Linda as
she stood before him.

She looked more at peace than she had earlier in the
café. Apparently her worries about Boots had been put
to rest. Her eyes were clear and her cheeks were rosy.
She had her golden-brown hair tied back in a ponytail
and silver earrings twinkled on her ears.

"It's Latin," Duane said as he smiled down at Linda. He was glad to see her looking good.

Linda frowned. "Shouldn't people be able to understand the words? It doesn't mean much if people don't know the words."

"The pastor recommended it," Duane said as he glanced over at Pastor Curtis.

"Well, yes, I guess," the pastor murmured.

"I suppose it's okay then. Does it come with a translation so I'll know what I'm singing?"

The pastor nodded. "Let me go get a couple of copies for you."

It took Duane and Linda ten minutes to get their music and settle themselves in front of the empty church. The pastor had left. Someone had left two of the old choir robes in the front pew for them.

"They'll need to be cleaned," Linda said. "But someone's probably going to Miles City in the next day or so. I can ask around."

Duane nodded. "Thanks. I'll pay for the cleaning, of course. And mileage, too, for whoever goes. Even some extra if they want."

"That would be appreciated." Linda gave him a smile. "Budgets are tight around here."

It was a perfect smile, but Duane didn't believe she meant anything by it. He'd almost rather see her genuine expression of rebuke than this polite smile. He wondered if he should keep her to her agreement to sing with him. She looked like a martyr on the way to a lonely jail cell somewhere. He knew she didn't want to sing with him.

Of course, Duane realized he couldn't afford to be

that generous. His voice wasn't strong enough yet to carry a song alone. He needed Linda if he was going to sing anything worth listening to.

Duane turned to the music and strummed a few chords on his guitar. He was playing a Martin guitar these days, the best instrument in the business in his opinion. The difference between this and his first guitar was equal to the difference between the mud-rutted lane leading to his great-aunt's house and the four-lane freeway leading to his house in Hollywood. The Martin guitar formed the notes effortlessly; his old Silvertone guitar needed to work for every sound it made.

Still, sometimes Duane missed the rough, plaintive sounds of that older guitar. He'd played jazz music sitting outside Chicago soup kitchens on that guitar and gotten a fistful of quarters each time. That guitar belonged to him in a way nothing else did. Not that he wanted that guitar around to remind him of those cold, hungry days.

"Are you going to read out the English words before we sing them in Latin?" Linda finally asked Duane. "I think it's important for people to know what they're listening to."

"Maybe we'll spell out some of the words at the end." Duane stopped strumming random chords and started to play the music in front of him.

Linda took that as her cue and started to sing. Duane had forgotten until that moment how rich her voice was. When they sang together in high school, she held the songs together with her lilting tones. Duane was content to accompany Linda for a while as she softly sang her way through the Latin song.

Linda said the words as though she meant them. And she must, because she insisted on knowing the translation for the Latin words. Duane wouldn't have cared if he was reciting a grocery list and he was impressed that Linda gave so much attention to what she was singing.

"You didn't do that back in high school," Duane finally said after they'd finished playing through the song a couple of times. "Back then you didn't care what the words meant."

Linda smiled and this time it took Duane's breath away. This smile was genuine. He'd never seen her look more beautiful.

"I want to praise God with the song. I didn't even know Him back in high school."

Duane nodded. He didn't really understand it all, but he was moved by her sincerity.

Just then the door at the back of the church opened and Lance walked inside. Duane saw his old friend standing there, with his hat in his hand, looking at the front of the church where Duane was.

"I think he wants to talk to you," Linda said quietly.

Duane got up and carefully put his guitar on a nearby pew. Then he walked to the back of the church. Lance's bruise showed up the closer Duane got to him. It was a toss-up as to who had the biggest shiner on his face, him or Lance.

"I came to apologize," Lance said gruffly when Duane got back to him. "I shouldn't have hit you like I did."

"You're apologizing? I'm the one who called you out."

Lance nodded. "Still, I should never have hit you."

"Well, I was going to hit you."

"I know. But you need your face for that press conference and I shouldn't have hit you, especially not there. The Bible tells us to turn the other cheek in times like those. That's what I should have done."

"Well…" Duane was speechless for a moment. "You mean you'd stand there and let me hit you and not hit me back?"

Lance nodded.

"Why?"

"I figure your decision to hit me was between you and God. My decision to hit you was between me and Him, too."

"But God doesn't care what I do."

"That's where you're wrong."

Duane just nodded at Lance when he got to that point. Duane didn't know what was happening to his old friends, but he felt as though they'd joined some special club and he was on the outside. He didn't like the feeling. Even when he thought that everyone else in Dry Creek looked at him as an outsider, he'd been sure Lance and Linda accepted him. Now, he didn't even have them.

"Well, thanks for coming," Duane said with what he hoped was a smile. "But I better get back to practicing."

Lance nodded and held out his hand.

Duane took his old friend's hand and shook it. He tried not to let his sadness show. Then Lance turned to leave the church.

Linda only had time to sing through the song one last time before she had to go back to the café. Duane thanked her as she gathered up her music and got ready to leave.

"Shall we meet earlier tomorrow?" Duane asked.

Linda nodded. "Ten-thirty would work better for me."

Duane hadn't realized he was holding his breath until Linda agreed to meet him again. Now that she and Lance were part of this special holy group, he wasn't too sure if Linda would still help him.

He'd never felt more alone, not even back in Chicago.

Duane put his guitar in its case and then sat down in one of the front pews. He was still sitting there when the pastor came up and sat beside him.

"How'd it go?" the pastor asked.

Duane shook his head. "I just don't understand the rules."

"Rules to what?"

"This Christian stuff." Duane turned to look at the pastor. "It seems like my friends refuse to be my enemies even when they should be. They just want to keep turning the other cheek until a body almost gives up in confusion. How's a person supposed to know who's on their side when people just keep turning that other cheek? One minute they're your enemies; the next minute they're your friends. Makes you wonder if they're either."

The pastor grinned. "Ah, you take me back. I used to ask those same kind of questions. I just didn't get it."

"You!" Duane was surprised. "You're a pastor. I thought you were just born in that special Christian club."

Pastor Curtis shook his head. "No one's born to it. God offers it to everyone, though."

"Well, that's no way to keep the troublemakers out."

"God doesn't want to keep the troublemakers out. He wants to bring them in just like everyone else."

"That's nice." Duane looked at the pastor. Obviously the other man had never had to survive on the streets of Chicago. No one wanted the troublemakers there. Half of the places didn't even want a young boy just because they thought he might cause problems. Duane didn't see any reason for God to be different than the authorities in Chicago. Of course, he wasn't going to sit here and argue with the pastor. Not with the press coming to town in a few days. So he added, "Real nice."

"Here, let me give you something," the pastor said as he reached into his pocket and pulled out a pamphlet. "This might answer some of your questions. And I'm always willing to talk to you. If I'm not at the church, I'm probably at the hardware store. I manage that for the owner these days."

Duane took the pamphlet with a polite smile. Not that he needed it. He only had to get along with people until Friday when the reporters came. It was Tuesday today. He should be able to keep things together for a few days without reading anything. He put the pamphlet into his shirt pocket and smiled again. "Thanks. I'll read it sometime."

Duane hoped God wouldn't strike him down for telling an outright lie in a church. Maybe God was into that turning the other cheek business, too.

The pastor nodded as he stood up. "It was easier for

me to understand when I saw it all laid out in black and white. It'll answer a lot of your questions."

Duane didn't want to give anyone the impression that he had any more spiritual questions, so he let the pastor walk away in silence. After a few minutes, Duane heard a low whining outside and he went to the door.

It was Boots. Duane marveled at how intelligent his dog was. Boots had found Duane at the church once before and so he'd looked there again.

Duane sat down on the steps and gave his dog a hug. Duane always knew where he stood with Boots.

"I wish I had a dog biscuit for you, old boy." Duane patted his dog.

Boots seemed content without the biscuit as long as Duane kept rubbing the dog's neck.

Duane wished his other old friends were as uncomplicated as Boots. His dog didn't want to apologize for anything and had no expectations for him. Duane leaned his head on Boots's neck and rested there for a moment. He'd noticed that Boots was walking slower than he had eight years ago. Maybe the dog wouldn't need so much exercise anymore. Duane wondered if there was any way he could bring Boots back to Hollywood with him. He knew it was selfish to want to take the dog to the city with him, but Duane could use a steady friend like Boots.

He was feeling lonely all of a sudden.

The odd thing was that Duane had never thought he needed anyone around him before. That's one of the things he'd liked about cities like Hollywood. He knew that it was easy to be invisible in the crowds there and time passed faster. He was used to that kind of a life.

He'd never made friends easily. People didn't usually offer him any friendship. And that was okay. Duane knew he had a tendency to frown and be suspicious of people. He'd learned the hard way that everyone was out for themselves. But he understood; he honestly never minded that.

Until lately. He felt he didn't know anything anymore. Ever since he'd started longing to sleep in his old bed in Great-Aunt Cornelia's house, nothing had been the same. He didn't get good cell phone reception and the quiet of not having a phone was surprisingly relaxing. He didn't even miss the lights and the big stores. He wondered if he was having some kind of a breakdown. Or maybe he just needed to take a sabbatical from his life.

All he knew for sure was that the days he was spending here in Dry Creek were the most pleasant days he'd spent in years. There was no applause and no one was offering him any record deals. But he found he liked knowing the names of the people he saw during the day. He wasn't buying stamps from a machine and passing strangers on the street. He actually knew people here. They might not be willing to accept him as someone who belonged here, but he found he liked knowing their names.

He gave Boots another hug and stood up. He needed to let Phil know that the song was going well. And then he'd find out what he needed to do to get his bus out of the middle of his driveway.

He should be getting ready to leave Dry Creek instead of daydreaming about staying.

Chapter Eleven

Linda decided to put a pie in the oven when she got back to the café after practicing with Duane. She had one in the freezer and she pulled it out to bake it. Her honorary grandfathers had been sitting drinking coffee and waiting for her to return. They said they were just finishing up breakfast, but she was not fooled. She was touched by their concern and she wanted to give them something to show her appreciation. She knew they wouldn't welcome a tearful thank-you speech, but they would each enjoy a piece of freshly baked blackberry pie.

A woman never went wrong by giving a man a piece of pie.

While Linda was in the kitchen putting the pie in the oven, the old men sat in the front part of the café and muttered amongst themselves.

"It's not right," Elmer fretted. He had an empty cup of coffee in front of him and he looked down at the handle. "That Duane Enger comes in here like he's the president or something and gets everyone all worked up when he knows all along that he's just going to leave again."

Charley nodded. He crumbled a cold piece of toast in his fingers. "I'm worried about Mrs. Hargrove. If Duane upsets Boots by leaving, I'm afraid Mrs. Hargrove will mope around, too. She's real fond of that dog."

Burt Jones looked up. "Are you starting to go sweet on Mrs. Hargrove or something?"

"What makes you ask a fool thing like that?" Charley scowled as he let go of the toast and looked at the other man.

Burt shrugged. "You just seem to worry about her a lot. That's all. She doesn't strike me as the kind of woman who needs someone worrying over her. You didn't use to worry."

"I'm worried about the *dog*. Can't a man worry about an animal around here? We're all retired farmers. We've spent our lives caring about animals. It's our job."

The other men looked at Charley, but they didn't comment.

Then they heard the sound of the kitchen door opening and they all tried to look as if they were still eating breakfast. Charley even managed to put a bit of that cold toast in his mouth. No one wanted Linda to think they were sitting here because they were worried about her.

"It'll be a while until the pie's ready," Linda announced as she walked over to their table. "But you've each got a piece of it on the house when it comes out of the oven. It's blackberry."

"Blackberry. That'd be real nice," Elmer said. "You're awful good to your customers."

"We're more than customers, more like family," Charley added.

Burt nodded. He had the sleeves of his flannel shirt rolled up to his elbow and he kept his coffee spoon in his hand. "Anything you need. You and your sister both. Call me. Anytime."

Linda nodded to them all. "I appreciate it. I—" Linda looked as though she was going to cry. "Excuse me, I need to get some more coffee going."

The old men watched Linda rush back to the kitchen.

"I don't suppose there's any way we could get Duane Enger to leave now before he does any more damage." Elmer looked miserable. "I know Linda said we shouldn't, but we have to do something."

"It's a free country," Burt muttered. "He's not going to leave just because we ask him to. Not with that press conference of his coming. The Enger boy has never been easy to push around."

Charley grunted. "What can you expect? He learned to stick up for himself in Chicago. He's a street fighter, all right. Remember how tough he acted when he first got off the bus in Dry Creek?"

Elmer nodded. "Everybody started locking their cars. We'd never done that before."

"Never had any reason to before," Burt muttered as he set his spoon on the empty plate in front of him.

Charley nodded. "I remember my wife—bless her soul—thought we were too hard on the boy. But I told her that a boy who gets caught trying to steal a car in Chicago isn't going to turn over a new leaf just because the courts make him move halfway across the country to a place like Dry Creek. Until the day she died, my wife stood up for that kid."

The men were silent for a moment, remembering the past.

"He never did steal a car here," Burt finally noted.

"It's because they were all locked up," Elmer said. "We didn't give him a chance to steal one from us. I remember I bought that Cadillac. A prime classic car if there ever was one. I kept an eye out for the Enger boy until the day he left town."

They were quiet and listened to the sounds of pans clinking together in the kitchen. They all knew Linda cooked when she was upset.

Elmer sighed. "Too bad we can't get the courts to move him this time."

"They can't just move people around to suit us. He hasn't done anything." Charley brushed the toast crumbs to the middle of his plate.

"He hit Lance," Burt offered.

All three men looked up and brightened.

"Do you think we could get Lance to press charges?" Elmer asked. He kept his voice down so it would not carry as far as the kitchen door. "I hear Lance has quite a shiner."

"So does Duane," Charley said. "But I heard Duane started it. It could be assault."

"Of course it's assault. That boy always was trouble."

"No one knows if the check he wrote for the youth group is good, either." Elmer put his elbows on the table and leaned toward the other men. "I wonder if it just might bounce when it hits the banks."

"I've never heard he was passing bad checks. But we could always ask Sheriff Wall to look into it," Charley added. "Sort of as a precaution."

"I don't think the sheriff's made his rounds through town yet today," Burt said.

The three men just sat and looked at each other.

"It wouldn't be very nice," Charley finally said. "I wonder if—"

Burt shook his head. "We're only protecting the women here—" Burt looked at Charley "—and the dogs. Men have always been the ones who look out for their—" he gave Charley another look "—dogs."

They were all quiet for another minute.

"Well, somebody does need to do something," Elmer finally said. "We're only raising the question. Nobody's hauling anyone off to jail. We're just being sensible."

The two men looked at Charley until finally he nodded. "Okay. We'll talk to Sheriff Wall."

Just then Linda came out of the kitchen with several glasses of iced tea. "You've all had so much coffee already, I thought you might like some of this herbal tea. It's good for you."

Ordinarily, the older men would refuse herbal tea, but they all felt so guilty they each took a glass and gulped down half of the tea before any of them said anything.

Finally, Charley set his glass down. "Thanks. That hit the spot."

"It's got lots of health benefits, too," Linda said.

All three of the older men nodded.

"I'll drink more of it later," Elmer lied.

* * *

Meanwhile, Duane was hiding in the bus. He knew Phil was in the house and wouldn't even think to look for Duane in the bus. Not that he was hiding from Phil in particular; Duane was hiding from everyone. That's why he was in the backseat of the bus where the windows were tinted the darkest.

He'd decided to read that pamphlet the pastor had given him. He didn't know why exactly. It's just that the thought had jumped into his head that maybe if he became a Christian he could change as much as Lance had changed.

The difference between the man Duane had seen lately and the boy he'd grown up with was huge.

Duane remembered the first time he'd met Lance. They'd both been boys. Lance had been dropped off by the Greyhound bus just as Duane had been some months earlier. Neither one of them had any luggage, just a few possessions dumped into a brown paper bag. And both of them wore expressions on their faces that dared anyone to comment on all that they didn't have.

Of course, Lance hadn't come from the city streets. He'd learned to fight on some Indian reservation in the Dakotas. Duane and Lance had understood each other almost from the beginning. They each knew they had no one to rely on except themselves.

But that had been almost twenty years ago.

And Lance had changed. Duane knew he'd told Phil that Lance wasn't a fit husband for Linda, but the truth was that Lance wouldn't be half-bad. The man had obviously learned a thing or two about relating to people. The other ranch hands seemed to like him and not just because they were afraid of him. His eyes looked kind these days.

Something had tamed Lance and Duane wanted to know if it was God. And, if God had done it for Lance, maybe there was hope for Duane after all. Of course, Duane didn't want to talk about this with anyone else. He didn't want anyone to look into his heart just as he hadn't wanted anyone to see inside that paper bag he'd carried off the Greyhound bus all those years ago. No one needed to know how little he had in either place.

Instead, he'd just take some time with that pamphlet and read about it.

The words on the pages were so simple Duane read them and wondered if that was all there was to this Christian stuff. There were a few Bible verses and instructions on what God expected before He made a person into a Christian.

There really wasn't much. Apparently all you had to do was to ask God to make you into a Christian and then read the Bible to find out what else to do.

Duane wondered if that could be all there was to it. His mind went back to that old Sunday school song he'd sung as a boy. He'd liked the simplicity of it as a boy. He let himself remember the words: "Jesus loves me, this I know, for the Bible tells me so."

It just didn't seem that it could be enough. Duane decided maybe he would need to talk to the pastor after all. He doubted he could keep it a secret if he did become a Christian anyway. For one thing, Lance would want to know. Duane had a feeling his old friend would be very happy with the news. In fact, Duane might just tell the whole town of Dry Creek if he made the leap.

The people here weren't really so bad. Maybe he'd been too sensitive as a boy to see that they were really rather friendly.

Duane thought on that for several minutes. Would the people of Dry Creek have gathered him to their collective heart if he'd been willing?

Duane heard someone knocking at the door of the bus. For a brief second, he wondered if God had brought the pastor to his door. He put the pamphlet down on the bus seat and stood up. If it was the pastor, Duane didn't want to keep him waiting.

When Duane opened the door, he didn't know if he was relieved or disappointed. The man there wasn't the pastor. Instead, the man wore a beige sheriff's uniform.

"Can I help you?" Duane asked.

"Just checking things out. I'm Sheriff Wall. Dry Creek is my territory."

The sheriff was trying to see inside the bus, but all he could see would be the driver's area.

Duane nodded. He knew Dry Creek had a county sheriff who came through now and again. He didn't recognize this man, though. "You must be fairly new."

The sheriff shook his head. "Been here awhile. Came shortly after you left, I think."

Duane decided he'd had enough trouble in Dry Creek. If he meant to make friends with the people here, he might as well start today. He held his hand out to the sheriff. "Well, it's good to meet you. I'm Duane Enger. Cornelia Enger's great-nephew."

Instead of shaking Duane's hand, the sheriff leaned forward so he could look down the length of the bus. "It's some vehicle you have here."

"Thanks," Duane said as he withdrew his hand. He tried not to be offended that the sheriff didn't want to shake hands. Duane figured maybe his voice still sounded strained and the sheriff thought he had a cold or something. "It's just my voice, nothing more. No germs."

The sheriff didn't even smile. "Where'd you get the bus?"

"We ordered it special. Straight from Detroit. Isn't she a beauty?"

"Who's we?"

"The band I'm with. We own it together."

The sheriff nodded. "I don't suppose you have some paperwork to prove that."

Duane stopped smiling. "You mean a registration?"

"Yeah. And a driver's license for it."

Duane realized the sheriff hadn't been worried about germs at all. "Is this a business visit?"

"Let's just say, I'm checking things out."

Duane reached over and opened the glove compartment. He pulled out some papers and then pulled out his wallet. "These should do it for you."

The sheriff took the papers and the wallet with the license. He looked them over before handing them back. "They seem to be in order."

"Trust me, no one steals a bus," Duane said as he put his wallet back in his pocket. *Not even me.*

"I'm just doing my job," the sheriff said. "No need to get your feathers all ruffled. When I heard you were back, I thought I'd see how you're doing."

"You don't even know me," Duane said. There was

something here that wasn't adding up and he didn't know what it was.

"Well, you know small towns," the sheriff said as he ducked his head. "People worry."

Duane froze in place. "Who's worried?"

The sheriff shrugged. "Just folks."

Duane felt the cold spread inside of him as he nodded his head. Apparently the good people of Dry Creek weren't as easy with him as he was beginning to hope.

"Was it Lance?" Duane asked.

"Naw." The sheriff shook his head. "But don't worry about it. Just keep things aboveboard and everything will be fine. I hear you're leaving soon anyway."

Duane nodded. Even if he had been thinking maybe he'd stay, he didn't have the stomach for staying where he wasn't wanted.

"Well, then, enjoy your time in Dry Creek," the sheriff said as he turned to leave. "Spring should be a good one this year. Too bad about the mud."

Duane didn't say anything as the sheriff turned and walked away from the bus.

Well, Duane thought to himself as he stepped down from the vehicle, he was glad he hadn't made a fool of himself by thinking there was hope for a man like him. There was no hope of changing when the people of Dry Creek were around to make sure he never forgot the past.

He watched the sheriff walk back to the main road where his car was parked.

Duane was a little surprised at the people of Dry

Creek. In the past, they did their dirty work themselves. They hadn't needed to call in the law to make sure he knew he wasn't welcome in their precious little town.

Chapter Twelve

Linda didn't know why Duane had stopped smiling. He'd stopped coming into the café. She thought Mrs. Hargrove might have brought him some groceries. The only time Linda saw him was when they practiced. But he wouldn't even smile when he sang that song they were working on for Sunday. He had the tortured doubting part down for the beginning and he sang that part with feeling. He didn't do so well on the hallelujahs at the end, though.

"You don't want to scare those reporters," Linda finally said. It was Thursday morning and technically they had the song ready. "Aren't you trying to tell them that you've had some sort of spiritual awakening?"

Duane growled. "They can take it or leave it."

"Okay," Linda said as she folded up her song sheets. "Well, Mrs. Hargrove took the choir robes in to be cleaned. She has them at her place."

"I can always count on Mrs. Hargrove."

"Yes," Linda said a little uncertainly. Duane made the

statement with so much feeling that she wondered if he meant something more by it. "You could always count on Lance and me, too."

Duane looked at her. "Really? When was the last time you saw the sheriff?"

"Sheriff Wall?"

Duane nodded.

Linda shrugged. "He came in the café a couple of days ago. He got a cup of coffee to go. Why?"

"I don't suppose you sat and talked to him about your worries."

"What's that supposed to mean? And if you're jealous, I'll have you know the sheriff got married a couple of years ago and he's a good family man."

Duane looked startled. "I wasn't jealous."

"Of course not," Linda said as she turned and took the song sheets to the front pew. Of course he wasn't jealous. She should leave before she embarrassed herself further.

"I mean…" Duane walked down to the pew, as well. "That is…"

Linda twirled around. "Don't you come near me."

She wondered if either one of them would be in shape to sing a song glorifying God on Sunday. Right now, she was sick and tired of Duane Enger. "And you stay away from Boots, too."

"My dog? What's Boots got to do with anything?"

"He's got a heart, too, you know," Linda said as she turned from the pew and started toward the center aisle.

"Hey," Duane said as he reached for her shoulder.

Linda stopped, but she didn't turn around. When she left here, she wanted to do so with dignity.

Duane kept his hand on her shoulder as he walked around to face her. "I'm sorry. I don't know what I've done wrong, but—please—I'm sorry."

Linda looked up at her old boyfriend. His eyes had lost all of their fierceness and he was looking softly bewildered.

Duane opened his arms to her and Linda went in to them as naturally as she had years ago. She blinked back the tears as he held her.

"I should…" Linda said after a minute. She stirred. She knew there was something she should be doing now, she just couldn't remember what it was. Oh, yes, the café.

Duane released her enough so they could stand face-to-face. He still kept his arms looped around her shoulders. She didn't want to look him in the eye so she focused on his chin.

"Your cuts have healed nicely," Linda said.

Duane put his hand on her chin and lifted her eyes to meet his. "I was trying to impress you with my clean-shaven looks."

Linda smiled.

Duane ran his thumb over her cheek. "Your skin's soft."

Linda wanted to ask how many women's faces he'd run his fingers over lately. She knew that someone who had so many fans had many invitations from women. She couldn't form the words, though. And, if the truth were told, Duane didn't look as if he was thinking about anyone but her.

He kissed her and she forgot about all of the other women, too.

After the kiss, Linda hid her face in Duane's shoulder for a bit.

"I haven't done anything wrong in Dry Creek," Duane whispered to her. "Or away from here, either. No one needs to worry about their cars."

"What?" Linda moved back so she could look at Duane's face. He looked as vulnerable to her as he did when he was a boy.

"Someone had the sheriff come and check me out," Duane said. "To be sure I hadn't stolen that bus."

"No one would steal a *bus*."

"I know." Duane kissed her on the nose. "But some people around here are worried anyway."

"Well, I can't imagine who that would be," Linda said before it occurred to her that she did know a few people who might be more worried than they needed to be. "Oh."

Duane lifted his eyebrow in question.

Linda shrugged. "I just thought of someone I should talk to—"

Duane was very still. "Is it Lance?"

"Don't be silly. Lance isn't worried about you. At least, not in that way."

Duane nodded. "I suppose not."

"Suppose nothing. Lance is your friend. He trusts you."

Duane looked at her. "And you?"

Linda swallowed. "I have no reason not to trust you. Not really."

Duane smiled. "I promise I'll answer all of the letters from Dry Creek myself from now on."

"Okay." Linda smiled. "I'll tell Lucy."

Duane nodded. "You could write, too, you know."

"I guess someone should write and tell you how the conference goes for the youth group."

"That's a start." Duane kissed her on the forehead.

"I need to get back to the café," Linda whispered.

Duane nodded and let her go. "I'll see you here tomorrow for our last rehearsal."

Linda turned and hurried down the aisle of the church. She welcomed the cool outside air as she opened the door. She didn't know if she felt doomed or elated. Duane wanted her to write to him. He'd practically promised to answer her letter if she wrote any and, one thing she could say for Duane, he kept any promises that he made.

She didn't know where letters would lead them, but it made her feel good inside just to think that she could pick up a pen and write a letter to him and he would read it. He wasn't totally lost to her, after all.

Duane watched Linda walk out of the church and he felt at peace with himself. He hoped he'd started to mend his friendship with Linda. They might never have anything deeper than friendship, but at least they would have that. His life already sounded better now that Linda was back in it.

Duane walked out of the church, too. He stood on the steps and looked around to see if Boots was going to meet him today, but apparently his dog was busy elsewhere.

The sky was overcast as Duane walked out of town. He had his jacket and it kept him warm in the chill. It looked as if it would rain soon and Duane thought he should finish digging some of the dried dirt out from around the wheels of the bus before it all turned back to mud.

It was funny how he could feel so much hope on an overcast day like today.

Duane saw the car before he reached the lane leading to his great-aunt's house. His first thought was that maybe one of the youth members from the church group was at the house hoping to arrange more work. If any of them were that enterprising, Duane would find something for them to do.

He'd never thought it would feel so good to help the kids in Dry Creek. He usually never stayed in one place long enough to care about the other people who lived around him, but he did want good things to happen for the people of Dry Creek, even if they were still nervous about him.

Duane wondered if he could ever get a new start in this small town.

A flash of lightning rolled through the sky as Duane walked down the lane. He hurried along. If it there was going to be a storm, he'd rather be in the house than in the bus. It started to rain before he reached the porch. Once he stood on the steps he stopped and took a deep breath. He'd always liked the musty earth smell that came with the Montana rains.

It thundered and Duane opened the door to the kitchen. He scraped his feet on the mat that sat on the linoleum by the door. His great-aunt had picked that welcome mat out and Duane liked knowing it was there. He wished the woman was around for him to still talk to about his problems. The two of them had understood each other.

Duane heard the sound of conversation in the living room and wondered if Phil had turned on the radio. Great-Aunt Cornelia had never owned a television, but she always had a radio that was powerful enough to pull in a wide range of stations.

When Duane reached the doorway of the living room he saw that Phil had company.

"Come meet Howard Mahr," Phil said as he gestured for Duane to come inside the room. "He's with the *Hollywood Reporter*."

"Freelance," Howard said as he stood and turned to offer Duane his hand.

Duane shook the man's hand. "Great."

It wasn't great, of course. Duane wondered what had possessed the man to come a day before any of the other reporters were scheduled to arrive. He knew the answer to that question before it was even fully formed in his mind. Freelancers were always a little more hungry for the story than the regular reporters were.

"I hope you're finding what you need," Duane said.

Phil gave him a funny look. "Howard wants to take a new angle."

The reporter nodded. "Not to minimize your thing at the church, but I want to do a different kind of an article."

Duane was getting a bad feeling in his bones. "Different?"

"I heard you've been having trouble with the law here," Howard said. "That's always something fans want to know."

"I don't know why," Duane snapped back. "It's some person's misfortune is all."

"So it's true?" Howard reached in his back pocket and pulled out what was probably a small recorder.

"Of course it's not true."

"I heard the sheriff had been parked out on the main street the other day. Heard he walked down and talked to you."

"Who told you that?"

"You know I can't say." Howard smiled smugly.

Duane looked at his manager. Some days the band didn't pay Phil enough. "You handle him."

Phil nodded. "We don't have the formal press conference until Sunday after church anyway."

Howard nodded. "I know that. I'll just get settled into town then. Where's a good hotel?"

"There are no hotels." Duane ground the words out. Maybe the man would take the hint and head back to Hollywood where he belonged.

"One of the locals, Mrs. Hargrove, has a room over her garage that she rents out," Phil said.

"Oh. How would I find that?"

Duane refused to answer that. He wasn't going to lead a snake like this man to the older woman.

"It's just down the street from the café," Phil finally said.

"She charges a hundred a night," Duane said. He'd call her and make sure she charged the man that. There was no reason to encourage this reporter to stay in Dry Creek.

Howard nodded. "Thanks."

Neither Phil nor Duane told the man he was welcome

for the information. They just watched him walk through the kitchen and back outside.

It was raining and they both knew the man didn't have an umbrella. Neither one of them cared.

"He's trouble," Phil said after a few minutes.

Duane nodded. "I figured as much."

"At least you're not applying for some choir someplace," Phil said with a weak smile. "I don't know how much damage he can do. No one cares about something that happened years ago anyway."

Duane didn't dispute that statement even though he knew that some people in Dry Creek apparently cared very much about things that had happened when he was a boy. He figured he might as well tell Phil what they faced. "There are people here who could say things about me."

Phil lifted an eyebrow in question. "Did you murder someone?"

"Of course not. They're worried about me trying to steal a car."

Phil relaxed. "As long as you're not going to jail, I don't think it will matter too much. You might want to soft-pedal the spiritual-awakening stuff on Sunday, though. You don't want them to say you're a hypocrite."

Duane looked at his manager. "Which is exactly what I am. But don't worry—they won't know it for sure unless any of them can speak Latin."

Duane hoped Linda wouldn't be too upset if he didn't tell people what the words to the song were that they were going to sing.

"Too bad it's not Greek," Phil said with a little smile.

Duane snorted. He couldn't remember the last time

the manager had attempted to make a joke. He didn't know if that should make him relax or worry even more.

"We'll do fine," Phil said. "I'll go around and talk to people tomorrow. See if I can guide them in their conversations with Howard."

Duane shrugged. "It might not do any good. The people here generally speak their mind."

"Don't worry. I haven't been in this business as long as I have without learning how to put a good spin on things."

"You shouldn't need to put a good spin on things. I didn't do anything."

Phil nodded. "But perception is key."

Duane supposed he couldn't argue with that. All he could hope for was that a few people in Dry Creek would support him. Well, maybe not support him, but be willing to tell the reporter that he wasn't a criminal or anything.

There was a sound on the porch and Duane walked to the door. When he opened it, he saw Boots wagging his tail. He knelt down and put his arms around his wet dog. It was too bad Boots couldn't talk to any reporters.

"Let me get you some biscuits," Duane said after a while. "Stay here until I come back."

Mrs. Hargrove had given him some dog biscuits for Boots and Duane pulled a handful of them out of the plastic bag and headed back outside.

"Here you go, boy." Duane held out the biscuits.

Boots came over to smell the biscuits, but then turned away.

"Somebody else has been feeding you, haven't they?" Duane said as he patted Boots.

One thing he could say for the people of Dry Creek, Duane thought to himself, is that they knew how to take care of pets. He knew that Boots could go to many different doors in this small town and get a handout. The people here may not have drawn him to their hearts, but they sure did take good care of his dog.

Maybe that's all he could ask of them, Duane thought.

Chapter Thirteen

Duane walked to the café the next morning. He'd thought about it and finally decided he wasn't going to let this town stand between him and Linda. If she was willing to be his friend again, he was going to see her. He figured he'd never have a chance to be more than a friend to her, but he wasn't going to throw away what he had.

He stopped to check the wheels on the bus as he passed the vehicle in the lane. The rainstorm last night hadn't dropped all that much moisture. The dirt around the wheels had gotten a little wet, but it wasn't the deep mud that had been present on the night when he'd gotten the bus stuck.

Really, he told himself, he should have dug the bus out earlier. He didn't know why he'd been content to leave it there. Maybe he hadn't wanted to leave Dry Creek anyway and the bus gave him an excuse to stay.

He'd need to be leaving on Sunday, though, after the press conference. Even if it was late afternoon, it would be time to leave when he'd finished with the reporters.

As far as he was concerned, the people of Dry Creek could say what they wanted about him then.

If what Phil said was true about the band attracting a large following south of the border, the guys didn't need to pin any hopes on this press conference anyway. Phil was always extra cautious about these things.

And Duane was beginning to realize he just didn't care that much about the future of the band. Oh, he wanted good things for the other guys. But, for him, it didn't matter.

The closer Duane walked to the café, the more his thoughts about the future grew. He hadn't had enough time to think about anything for years it seemed. Now that he had time, he was realizing he wanted to make some changes in his life.

He took a deep breath and let the thought fill his head. He wanted to quit the band.

For the first time, he understood why the former band members had decided to give it up. In these past few days he'd gotten a taste of community and home. He liked it. Of course, the community in Dry Creek wasn't his community, but there were other small towns. He might find one that suited him as he drove the bus back to Hollywood.

He'd like to have mornings again. When they were on tour, he and the other band members were too tired from the night before to enjoy mornings. He might even like to find a church someplace that would teach him more about God.

He remembered his great-aunt Cornelia. He was sure she would agree with his decisions if he had a chance to talk to her. She'd always wanted him to slow down and smile a little. To make some friends. To live with peace in his heart. To be content with a good, honest life.

Duane was on the porch of the café almost before he knew it. He unzipped his jacket slightly and slicked back his hair. At least he'd been able to shave properly this morning.

Duane opened the door and stepped inside. He braced himself for the old men, but the room was empty until Linda came out of the kitchen with a pot of coffee in her hand.

"Hi." Duane walked over to a table.

"I thought you'd started doing your own cooking," Linda said as she walked over to his table. "Coffee?"

"Please." Duane smiled. "I'd be a fool to eat my cooking when you've got the café here."

Linda smiled back.

Duane told himself that smiling was a good beginning for the two of them. That's where they'd started back in junior high school.

"Where's everybody?" Duane asked as he looked around.

Linda shrugged. "I don't know. Mrs. Hargrove was just here, but then she left. Usually the grandfathers are all here by now."

"Grandfathers?"

"It's just what Lucy and I call them."

Duane nodded. He hadn't realized until that moment that Linda and Lucy had felt so alone that they had invented relatives. He knew that they would miss their mother, but he'd never thought of them not having real grandparents or aunts and uncles. At least he had had his great-aunt. "I'm sorry I've been gone."

Linda looked at him cautiously.

"You needed your friends and I wasn't here."

"It's okay," Linda said softly as she pulled out her order pad. "What'll it be?"

Duane resisted the impulse to throw his heart at her feet. "Scrambled eggs and toast."

Linda nodded and went back to the kitchen.

Duane turned around and looked through the big window in the front of the café. He saw Mrs. Hargrove going into the hardware store. Now what could the woman want in there at this hour of the morning?

Charley tipped his coffee cup back and took another drink even though it tasted a little metallic.

"Who cleaned the pot last?" Elmer asked as he looked down at his own cup.

"*When* is my question." Burt set his cup down on the empty wooden chair next to him. He'd only taken one swallow of the coffee. "There's something wrong with it."

The three men were sitting around the old wooden stove in the middle of the hardware store. They usually spent their afternoons here and had already drunk their daily coffee quota by then. No one had made coffee in the pot on the counter for some time.

"I didn't get breakfast, either," Charley grumbled as he took another gulp of the coffee in his cup.

The windows of the hardware store looked out onto the only street in Dry Creek, but no one paid any attention to them. Industrial shelves stood to one side of the large room and held bins of nails and screws.

"Well, I guess we could go back to the café. It's not like Linda knows what we've done," Elmer said.

The three men just looked at each other and grimaced. They all knew they felt too guilty to go back to the café right now. They were silent for a minute. The hardware store was empty presently. The pastor was working in the back stockroom so he couldn't hear them.

"I'm wishing we hadn't done it," Charley finally muttered. "I miss having eggs for breakfast."

"Me, too," Burt said with a sigh.

"Well, you're the one who thought we should do it in the first place," Elmer snapped as he turned to Burt. "We wouldn't have even thought of sending the sheriff out there if you hadn't been going on about it."

"Me? I thought it was you."

Charley raised his hand. "No one's more to blame in this than the others. We're all at fault."

Elmer looked like he wanted to protest that statement, but he didn't.

They all looked over at the door in relief when they heard it open and Mrs. Hargrove came inside. The older woman had a wool scarf wrapped around her head and rubber boots on her feet.

"So here you all are." Mrs. Hargrove unzipped the heavy jacket she wore. "I thought you'd all be over at the café having breakfast."

"We don't go there every day," Charley said.

"Of course you do." Mrs. Hargrove slid off her boots. "Unless you're visiting at my house, that is."

"Oh," Charley mumbled.

"I was just wondering why you're not there," Mrs. Hargrove said as she walked closer to the stove.

The three men exchanged alarmed looks.

"We're on a diet," Elmer blurted out.

Mrs. Hargrove stopped and looked at the men skeptically.

"The doctor said we should cut back on the cholesterol," Burt added. He stared straight ahead at the stove.

"Well, you still have to eat." Mrs. Hargrove spread her hands out to the stove and then pulled back in surprise. "No one lit a fire in this thing."

"We're conserving heat," Elmer said.

By now, all of the men were looking flushed.

Mrs. Hargrove nodded. "You'd conserve even more heat if you were over at the café—" she paused "—having a nourishing bowl of hot oatmeal. That lowers the cholesterol, you know."

All three men nodded, but none of them moved.

Mrs. Hargrove sat down in one of the empty chairs and looked around. She hadn't taught decades of Sunday school classes for nothing. "Now, suppose you tell me why you're really not at the café."

No one said anything.

"We were just trying to protect the town." Elmer finally broke. "We're not the criminals here. That Enger boy stole cars before he even got to Dry Creek."

"It was practically our civic duty to ask the sheriff to go check on him and that bus," Burt added. "We don't want anyone driving stolen vehicles into our town."

There was a moment's silence, then Charley said, "We're sorry we ever mentioned it to anyone."

"I should hope so," Mrs. Hargrove said. Her eyes

flashed. "How you could bring something like that up now, I don't know."

"We didn't think he was a good influence on—" Elmer began and then stopped. "Anyone."

"I don't know how you can say that."

"Well, he was sent here because he tried to steal a car," Elmer said in his defense.

"Oh, dear." Mrs. Hargrove shook her head. "If I'd known people were still going on about that, I would have told you all years ago what really happened. It's just I didn't know until Cornelia was so sick and, by that time, there didn't seem to be any point in rehashing it."

The men were silent. They were starting to look a little pale.

Finally, Charley got brave enough to ask. "Rehashing what?"

Mrs. Hargrove looked at the men. "That car Duane was trying to steal in Chicago. He wasn't trying to drive it anywhere. He just wanted to be able to get his mother inside it. It was bitter cold that night and the heater had stopped working in her car. He was only eleven. He broke a side window and opened it up."

"Oh," Charley said.

"It was just for the heat." Mrs. Hargrove shook her head. "The police even said in their report that he hadn't looked like he was going to take it anyplace. That's why the judge took pity on him and sent him here."

The men turned and looked at each other.

"Well, why didn't anyone tell us that years ago?" Elmer sputtered. "Here I was all worried about that Cadillac of mine. I didn't know he wasn't really going to steal anything back in Chicago."

Mrs. Hargrove shrugged. "I don't know if Cornelia thought it was better not to tell anyone. You know her. She didn't believe in making excuses. I don't think she would have told me, but she wanted to give me a copy of the documents she had on it before she died."

"Well, it would have been helpful to know," Charley said.

"It shouldn't have mattered to anyone this long after the whole thing happened anyway," Mrs. Hargrove said firmly. "People are supposed to be able to forgive people and move on. No one should hold on to their old misconceptions that long."

None of the men had anything to say to that. Elmer got so nervous he drank his entire cup of coffee, straight down at one time. He gulped a few extra times when it was all done, but he didn't complain.

"Well," Charley said, "I guess the only thing to do is to try to make it right by the boy."

"I can set it straight with Sheriff Wall," Burt offered.

All three men nodded.

"I guess I can talk to Duane and apologize," Elmer said a little slowly. "If he'll listen to me."

"I don't know why he'd forgive us now," Charley said glumly. "We haven't been neighborly to him in the past."

"It's never too late to change the way you treat someone," Mrs. Hargrove declared. "I tell my Sunday school class that all of the time."

"But those are little kids," Burt protested.

Mrs. Hargrove just looked at him. He had the grace to blush.

* * *

At the café, Linda was pouring a second cup of coffee for Duane. Since her morning business was so light, she poured herself a cup of coffee, too, and joined him. She and Duane were reminiscing about high school. Linda even told him about the outdoor concert the local kids had organized last year at the old stop sign by his place.

Duane kept asking questions.

Linda knew he was just trying to keep her relaxed so she would be able to do well singing with him on Sunday. She didn't care so much why he was doing it, though. All she hoped for from Duane was that this time, when he left, they could part as friends. She didn't want to carry the tight, teary feelings around in her anymore that came most of the times when she thought of him.

She wanted to be able to look at his old guitar that was hanging on the café wall and remember the good times they'd had. Linda found her eyes straying over to the guitar and Duane joined her in looking.

"I'm glad you have that here," Duane said. "That old guitar meant a lot to me. I played it many nights. It helped my mother sleep easy."

"You should have it with you. Anytime you want to take it, just let me know."

"It would get knocked around in the bus." Duane stood up and walked over to where the guitar hung. He took it off the wall and brought it back to the table. "Remember this song?"

Duane played jazz the way he used to play.

Linda felt she was eighteen again as she listened to the smooth notes. She started to hum a little to the music. Her heart healed a little with each measure of music Duane played. She had no desire to be angry with him anymore. He had gone away from Dry Creek to make his future. She had to accept his decision. She had made her own choices. She needed to let him go. God was good to her; He'd given her another chance to say goodbye to Duane Enger in a better way.

Chapter Fourteen

Duane gave himself a close shave. It was Friday morning and all of the reporters would be pulling into Dry Creek. He couldn't hide so he decided to put on a brave face and talk to them. Before he talked to anyone today, though, he wanted to talk to the pastor.

Duane had spent the afternoon yesterday getting the bus pulled out of its mud-encrusted rut. As he was digging out the old dirt, his mind kept returning to the pamphlet that was sitting on the backseat in that bus. He wondered if that old dried mud was some kind of a metaphor for his life.

Finally, he went into the bus and started the engine. He gunned the motor and the bus jumped forward. He drove the bus down to the house. He was in no hurry to go into the house so he sat down and read that pamphlet through several times. Every time he read it the longing inside of him grew. He wanted to have the kind of faith it talked about in those pages. He had no idea what his life would look like then.

The more he thought about his life, the more confident he was about his decision to leave the band. He was lonely and he was tired. Being in the band didn't make him happy. And, if he was going to leave the band to search for a more meaningful life, he might as well go all the way and ask God to give him the kind of rich life Lance and Linda were enjoying.

That's what he wanted.

But he wasn't sure the pamphlet had everything right. That's why he wanted to talk to the pastor. He wanted to do it right.

In the meantime, he would do what he could to keep the rest of the band looking good. And, he would do what he could to leave Dry Creek in peace.

He'd always had such a strained relationship with the town. He wanted their acceptance so much that he kept pretending he didn't want it at all. Only his great-aunt had seen through him. And maybe Mrs. Hargrove.

Even though Linda and Lance had been his friends in high school, they would be astonished to know that he had craved the good wishes of the people of Dry Creek back then and still wanted them today. His two friends no doubt thought he was itching to get away from the smallness of the place.

He'd been all over the country and he'd trade roots in a small town like this for the open road any day.

All of those thoughts had run through his mind last night as he went to sleep. He woke up convinced that leaving Dry Creek this time would be hard, but that he would do it anyway. He wanted to find a place to put down roots where people wanted him. There had to be another Dry Creek somewhere.

Duane didn't pass Phil in the kitchen as he left the

house. He was determined to take away some good memories when he left town this time. One of those memories would be of having breakfast with Linda in the café. He hoped that the old men weren't there this morning. He liked talking with Linda alone. He wanted to see her smile at him some more.

Linda couldn't make coffee fast enough. When she'd opened the café this morning at seven o'clock, there had already been a line of people waiting to get in. She never had a line and here she had hoped that this morning would be quiet. She wanted more time with Duane as she'd had the morning before.

And she was sick. She hadn't been sure she had a fever when she left the house, but she was becoming more convinced of it as time went on. But Lucy was in school and there was no one else to look after the café. She'd put a notice on the door warning everyone that she was coming down with a cold and that they came inside at their own risk.

That didn't even slow anyone down. The reporters who were here demanded breakfast. They'd slept in their cars and they all knew there was nowhere else in town to eat. So they ignored her worries.

Instead, they ordered as if they hadn't eaten for a week.

The reporter with the laptop wanted a short stack of pancakes and three slices of bacon as soon as possible. And real butter and jelly instead of maple syrup. And a side of hash browns.

The other reporter, who was bald and looked thoroughly bored, wanted an omelet with mushrooms in it and nothing else, not even cheese. And a single slice of wheat bread, warmed but not toasted. She didn't have time to debate with him whether he was ordering an omelet or just an egg with some mushrooms in it, because he was impatient, too.

And then Howard, that reporter who had been here for days begging people to say something outrageous about Duane, came through the door asking if she had fresh-squeezed orange juice to go. And, maybe, some toast to eat in the café. The reporter sat down and asked if he could see a menu.

"I'm sick," Linda said for the third time this morning.

The reporter eyed her suspiciously. "You look okay to me. Besides, there's nowhere else to eat in this town."

Linda pulled a small paper menu out of the pocket of her chef's apron and put it on the table in front of the man. She tried to convince herself that she should be happy for all of the business. In Dry Creek, a café owner had to take her customers when they showed up. She just didn't know why everyone needed to show up now. She'd taken a decongestant and an aspirin and she was feeling pretty good considering, but…

"Coffee?" Linda held the pot over the cup at the place setting where the reporter sat looking at the menu.

The reporter nodded his head.

"Make mine a soft-boiled egg and a slice of ham," he finally said as he opened up the journal he held. "And maybe some hash browns. Thin sliced."

"We only have one kind of hash browns."

"Oh, well, okay then."

Linda set the coffeepot on the table and made some notes on her order pad.

She expected the grandfathers to come in any minute now and she wanted to have all of the reporters served and out of her café by then. The one reporter, Howard, had made no secret of his desire to put Duane in a bad light in whatever he wrote. He'd been asking questions since he got to Dry Creek.

Linda was tempted to refuse service to the man. Him and his extra-thin hash browns and fresh-squeezed juice. They were in the middle of Southern Montana. They were lucky she served them anything that was fresh.

"Duane owns half this café, you know," Linda said as she put her notepad back in her pocket. Maybe the man would think twice before he expected special service here. She felt better just knowing he knew she stood in Duane's corner.

Howard nodded.

Just then the café door opened. A gust of cold air came inside.

"Duane," Linda said as she gave him a big smile. She wanted the reporters to know that Duane had at least one friend in Dry Creek, even if she was getting sicker by the minute. "Come on in. No, don't come in. I think I have a cold."

"No!" Duane looked stricken. "The doctor told me I wasn't contagious."

"I think it was the pastor's twins," Linda said. "They came by yesterday and I gave them some cookies. Their mother came by later and said they were in bed with colds today."

"Hey." The bald reporter held up his cup. "Could I get some more coffee here?"

"Wait your turn," Linda said as she held up her empty coffeepot.

Linda turned to Duane. "I'll be back after I put the pancakes on to cook and get some coffee for that one."

Linda jerked her head in the direction of the bald reporter before turning and walking into the kitchen.

Duane looked around the main part of the café again. There were the three reporters and a couple of ranch hands all sitting at tables and waiting for food. He could hear Linda in the kitchen getting a pan down from the cupboard.

He didn't know how they could all sit there demanding their breakfast when Linda didn't feel good.

Duane walked back to the doorway to the kitchen. "I can man the stove or get the orders—whichever you want."

"What?" Linda looked up from cracking an egg in a small bowl.

"I can cook or I can be the waiter," Duane repeated. "You look like you could use some help."

"Oh, I could."

Duane looked at Linda's face a little closer. She was flushed pink and her eyes were feverish. "In fact, I'll do both. You go home and get some rest."

"I couldn't do that," Linda said. "I have to keep the café open."

"I can do that. You need to go home and take care of yourself."

Linda looked over at him. "But you need to get ready for your press conference. And we need to practice again and—"

Duane shook his head. "Everything will be fine."

Linda stared at him for a minute and then she moved away from the stove. "Thank you."

"Don't worry about anything," Duane said as Linda took off her apron and hung it on a rack by the door.

"I'll come back after I rest a bit," Linda said as she opened the back door to the café and stepped outside. A gust of cold air came into the kitchen. And then the door closed.

Duane looked around. He went over to the coatrack and draped one of the white aprons over his neck. As he reached behind to tie the apron on, he looked at the rest of the kitchen. Linda had a commercial-grade stove with a large griddle area on the left side of the room. A freezer stood on the right. It looked used, but probably worked good. There were checkered curtains at the two windows and a large counter by a deep sink.

"Hey, out there," someone called from the main part of the café.

"Hold your horses," Duane said as he stepped over to the stove and slid the egg from the bowl to the griddle. A piece of toast popped up from the toaster on the counter.

There was a big bowl with some kind of batter in it. He spooned some of it onto the griddle.

Yeah, he could do this, Duane thought to himself as he remembered the coffee.

There was a coffeemaker next to the stove and it looked as if it already had a full pot of coffee just waiting to be poured.

Yeah, he could do this just fine, Duane told himself

as he picked up the pot of coffee and headed for the waiting customers.

Five minutes later, he was opening the windows so the smoke could escape.

Ten minutes later, he was serving pancakes to the bald reporter. "I wanted dry toast. Thin wheat dry toast."

"Well, you got pancakes," Duane said as he put a jar of syrup down on the table next to the plate of pancakes.

"But they're burned," the reporter protested.

"So's the toast," Duane replied. "And your egg got scrambled."

"Where's my orange juice?" Howard, the reporter Duane decided he didn't like at all, asked.

"I fed it to the cat," Duane lied. The truth was he'd saved it because he meant to take it out to Linda as soon as the breakfast rush was over. She needed her vitamin C.

"But I can't drink milk," Howard said.

"Good. We're out of milk. You can have water or coffee."

Duane felt he'd done pretty good serving the coffee. He'd only spilled a few drops of the scalding brew and then only when he was serving Howard.

"No, no coffee." Howard put his hands up. "This is my last clean shirt."

"Ah," Duane said as he looked over the other diners. "Anyone else need anything?"

There was silence for a minute.

"Could I have a fork?" a timid voice finally asked. It was one of the ranch hands from the Elkton place. Duane had just presented him with one and a half crispy fried eggs. "I can't eat without one."

Duane walked over to one of the empty tables and grabbed a place setting. He took it over to the ranch hand. "There. See. We can do this if we all work together."

Duane smiled at his customers. He hadn't gotten any complaints from the ranch hands and the reporters who were eating here were just spoiled in his opinion. He wondered if they even realized how hard it was to give everyone what they wanted in a café.

"We'll be closed from eleven to twelve," Duane announced. "You're all welcome to come back at twelve for sandwiches."

"What kind of sandwiches?" the bald reporter asked suspiciously.

"Tuna and peanut butter," Duane said. He figured he could handle both of those.

"Not together?" The reporter turned a little green.

"Of course not," Duane answered. "They'll be especially prepared by the café staff."

Duane figured he was getting the hang of this food business. "Now, if everyone would just take their plates back to the table closest to the kitchen, we'll be ready to close for our break."

Everyone stood up and carried their plates back.

Duane wondered if Linda shouldn't adopt some of his energy-saving steps. One person shouldn't be expected to fetch and carry for all of these people. If someone had difficulty walking, that would be different. But all of these men seemed able to carry a plate and coffee cup.

The café was clear and ready to close at eleven o'clock. Duane bottled up the orange juice for Linda and made her some dry toast. He was almost getting the hang of the toaster and decided he might offer a toasted tuna sandwich as a lunch special.

It took Duane a few minutes to go get the bus and drive it over to the café, but it didn't take long to load up his provisions. He even added some of those lozenges the doctor had given him in case Linda could use them.

The bus did surprisingly well on the road out to the Morgan place now that the roads were fairly dry. It hadn't rained at all for the past couple of days. The grass was coming in all along the way and there were splotches of green in the brown landscape.

Linda answered the door on Duane's second knock.

"Don't worry," Duane said. "I've got the café under control. I just closed for an hour so I could bring you a few things you'll need."

Duane handed her the bottle of orange juice and a white bag. "There's toast and tea bags in here and some prescription lozenges for your voice, too. They sure helped me."

"Oh." Linda looked up at him after she set the things on a wooden bench by the door. "I forgot about the song. I'm sorry. I'll start taking the lozenges right now. Maybe my voice won't sound so bad by Sunday."

"Don't worry about the song," Duane said. He was surprised he hadn't even given that any thought himself. "I'll figure it out."

"I'm not sure you can sing that song by yourself," Linda said. "Maybe Lucy could learn it. Her voice is just as good as mine."

"Don't worry," Duane said. He knew no one could

learn that song by Sunday. Besides, when he thought about it, he'd wanted to sing the song with Linda because it was Linda. It wouldn't be the same with anyone else.

"I don't want to let you down," Linda said.

Linda's hair was sticking out in all directions. Her lips were pale. Her eyes were red. Her skin was too white.

"You've never let me down," Duane said and he leaned in to kiss her on the forehead.

"I'm sick," she said, but she looked pleased all the same.

"I'm not worried," Duane said as he opened his arms and gave her a big hug.

"I promise I'll come on Sunday."

"I'd love to see you there," Duane said. "But not to sing. I'd just like to have you there if you can make it."

"I want to come," Linda said.

Duane held her for a moment and then he said, "I have to get back for the lunch hour. Those reporters will complain if they miss a meal."

"There's no other place to eat in Dry Creek."

"I know." Duane released her and stepped back. "That's the only reason I have pity on them."

The ride back to Dry Creek in the bus went as quickly as the ride out to Linda's had gone. Duane figured it was because he was trying to figure out how to make the tuna spread for a sandwich. Surely, his great-aunt had made tuna sandwiches. He must have seen her do it. He'd figure it out.

Chapter Fifteen

Sunday morning was overcast and Duane didn't want to get out of bed. This was the day of the press conference and he figured the reporters that were here already knew him too well. He'd been their cook and waiter for two days now and he'd even promised to open up the café for an hour before Sunday school started. He was serving French toast for breakfast. Howard claimed he knew the recipe and had offered to help him out in the kitchen this morning.

The need to eat drew men together. It just didn't make them respect each other.

Duane figured the reporters had no idea what to say about him by now. Phil had fed them several press releases all about how popular the band was and how much more popular they were going to be with their new fans south of the border.

Several of the old men in the town had tried to get the reporters alone to give them their opinions, too. Duane had managed to prevent any editorializing in the café, but he was sure some of the townsmen had spoken their piece as the reporters walked back and forth from their cars. He'd asked Howard what the old men were saying about him, but all Howard would say is that they were impressed with how nice Boots had turned out.

Of course Boots was a nice dog. Duane didn't know whether the old men were worried he might take Boots with him to Hollywood and wanted to prevent it or what their goal was. He would never want Boots to be unhappy so they didn't have to worry about him ending up in Hollywood. Duane did figure that the nice small town he was hoping to find would be a good place for Boots. He would pick a town with a functioning post office, too, because he planned to write Linda a letter as soon as he had a new address. He didn't know if he would ever be able to pry Linda away from Dry Creek, but he intended to try.

There was one thing he needed to do before he left Dry Creek and he planned to do it today. He'd met with the pastor yesterday after the café closed and the man had answered all of his questions.

Duane just needed to gather his courage and tell people that he'd become a Christian. He didn't know why it should matter to him that the people in Dry Creek knew about his new faith, but it did. This might not be the place God wanted him to set up a home, but it was still the place that had started the longing in his heart to have a home. He owed the people of Dry Creek the knowledge that they had made a big impact on his life.

And he wanted Linda to know. And Lance.

They had both said they would be at the church for his press conference. Linda was still worried about who was going to sing with him, but Duane had decided what he was going to do. He didn't have time to learn any new songs. He didn't have enough of his voice back to sing the song he and Linda had practiced.

But he did have a plan.

First, he had to make French toast for the reporters. He might even offer them some of his special tuna sandwiches in a to-go bag so they'd be prepared for lunch.

Linda woke up and went to the mirror in her bedroom. She opened her mouth and tried to sing. She had prayed for a miracle to restore her voice, but when the squeak came out she knew God hadn't done anything yet. She looked back at the clock beside her bed. She had three more hours before the duet was scheduled. She'd keep praying while she drank some hot lemon and honey water.

She had her first cup of the hot liquid while Lucy fixed her hair. The two of them sat in the kitchen. The smell of wheat toast was in the air from breakfast. Linda had finished the last of the orange juice Duane had brought over two days ago.

"I think an updo is what you need today," Lucy said as she swept Linda's hair up.

"Just simple," Linda croaked out. She was sitting on one of the kitchen chairs and she was wearing her oldest fuzzy robe.

"You'll want to put your best foot forward," Lucy said as she softly twisted Linda's hair. "Mama always said we were beautiful girls and we needed to let our light shine."

Linda turned her head so she could look up at her

younger sister. The lemon water was working because she could talk even if her voice was raspy. "Mama never said anything about us."

Lucy kept smoothing Linda's hair into the style.

Linda wondered if her sister had understood what she'd said. "I'm sorry, I—"

Lucy put a clip in Linda's hair and stood back. "There. That looks good."

Linda turned fully around so she could face her sister. She began again. "I'm sorry." Linda stopped to clear her throat. "I kept telling you things, but—"

Lucy looked at her.

Linda swallowed. "But Mama never said them."

Lucy smoothed Linda's hair back and then smiled at her. "I always wondered why I never remembered Mama talking to me."

"She would have, I think," Linda said. "But—"

Lucy shook her head. "Don't feel bad. It's okay. You talked to me."

"Me?"

Lucy nodded. "All of those things you told me mama said, I always figured it was you saying them to me anyway."

"Really?"

"Yes."

Lucy gave Linda's hair a final sweep. "There. It's perfect."

Linda couldn't believe it was that simple to set things straight with Lucy.

And her hair was perfect, Linda decided later as she stood in front of her mirror. She was dressing so that, if a miracle occurred and God healed her voice, she could sing with Duane. She was wearing her best white blouse so it would look good with the choir robes. And she had polished her black flats. And she'd used some midnight-blue mascara on the tips of her eyelashes.

She was ready to shine if God wanted her to.

Linda's voice was scratchy, but she felt fine other-wise. She gathered her coat and purse and told Lucy she could drive the car when they went to church. Linda was going to support Duane as best as she could this morning. And then she was going to let him go.

When Linda got to the church, she went into the room where the choir stored their robes. She figured Mrs. Hargrove would have hung the two cleaned robes on the hooks there and she had. The white collars on the robes were frayed a little and the blue color had a dif-ferent shine in some places where it was worn a little more than other places. But the robes would certainly make Duane look as if he belonged in a church.

Linda swallowed and quietly tried her voice again just to see if she could, through some miracle, sing now. All she heard was a hoarse squeak. Even the lozenges Duane had dropped off did not seem to be working on her voice.

Linda decided she would sit in the front row to support Duane anyway. She could mouth the words to him if he got lost in all of that Latin. At least she knew the song.

When she walked back into the church foyer, she saw that the pews were filling up. None of the reporters were here yet, though. Maybe they didn't intend to come for the church service, but just planned to come for Duane's song and press conference. Linda didn't think that was very sporting of them, but she supposed they were off working on other stories.

She had almost started up the aisle of the church when Charley motioned for her to come over to him.

"Hi," Linda said.

"Do you know where Boots is?"

"No, why?"

The older man frowned a little. "I'm just trying to find him. That's all. I thought some of the reporters might like to see how he acts when he first sees Duane. All that tail thumping and wagging. That dog is sure happy to see Duane. And I've never known a dog to take to a man who was no good. The mark of a man is how well his dog likes him."

"Well, I'm sure Boots is around here somewhere," Linda said. She didn't know why it was so important that Charley see the dog right now. "Maybe he's after a rabbit or something."

"Not Boots," Charley protested. "It's Sunday."

Linda didn't see the need to tell Charley that Boots didn't care what day of the week it was. Besides, she didn't see any of the reporters sitting in the pews yet. So Linda nodded to Charley and walked down the aisle. Usually she sat about halfway back, but today she continued to the very front.

Pastor Curtis seemed to be especially cheerful and preached a good sermon on God's faithfulness. Linda took a few notes. She'd been making it a habit to take notes in the sermons; it helped her concentrate better. Today she needed all of the help she could get just to stay focused. She didn't see Duane. She wondered if he'd gotten in that bus of his and driven right out of town. After all, there was nothing to keep him here but the reporters and they hadn't shown up yet, either. Maybe they'd all left together.

Duane was sitting in the back pew. He'd slipped in late because Howard was demonstrating how to make a flaming dessert he'd had in New Orleans. Of course, all he'd done was singe his own tie. The reporters promised they'd be at the church before it was time for Duane's solo, but they wanted to fix Howard's tie before then.

"I don't care about ties," Duane had said as he shooed them out of the café and made one last trip back through the place before leaving by the kitchen door. He'd picked up his old guitar on the way through and, all during the pastor's sermon, Duane had held the neck of that old guitar. When he thought of faithfulness, Duane thought of this guitar. He'd played it many a cold night in Chicago as he waited for a car to heat up or the soup kitchen to open. He used to wonder if the hoarseness of the guitar was there because it had endured so many freezing nights with him.

When the pastor finished his sermon, he announced that they were going to have a special musical number today by Duane Enger.

Duane stood up and, even though he was at the back of the church, he saw the relief in Linda's eyes when she turned around and saw him. He gave her a little smile. He was halfway up the aisle before he saw her confusion.

She was wearing a choir robe; he was not.

It made him feel good to know that she was doing all

she could for him as he got ready to perform. He'd decided the song he had to sing didn't need a choir robe. It didn't even need his expensive Martin guitar. What it needed was his faithful old Silvertone.

Duane pulled a chair into the middle of the raised platform at the front of the church and positioned two microphones near it. One was for the guitar, the other was for his voice. He could hear the shuffling in the pews. Everyone was craning their necks to see the performance. He looked out at the people. He'd known most of these people when he was a kid. Some of them had been on the streets of Dry Creek when he stepped off that Greyhound bus. They might not have warmed up to him then, but they had been important to him. He hoped he didn't disappoint them now. They were expecting a performance worthy of a rock star. But they weren't getting it. Instead, they were getting the song of his heart.

Duane started by strumming a simple chord. Then he began to sing.

"Jesus Loves Me,
This I know,
For the Bible Tells Me So.
Little Ones to Him Belong,
They are Weak, but He is Strong.
Yes, Jesus Loves Me. Yes, Jesus Loves Me.
Yes, Jesus Loves Me. The Bible Tells Me So."

Duane let the chords fade away. He saw the reporters sitting in the last pew of the church. They all had notepads in their hands, but none of them were writing anything. He wondered if he'd disappointed everyone. And then the church erupted in applause.

Linda blinked. She had been so worried and God had made things so right. The sincerity on Duane's face had been something to see as he sang his song. She blinked again.

Everyone was leaving the church and shaking Duane's hands. She found herself standing in line with everyone else. Then Lance was walking beside her and reached over to give her a big hug.

Linda told herself that, while she had been praying for a miracle so she could sing with Duane, God had a bigger miracle in mind for today.

She put her hand out when she reached Duane, but he did not shake it. Instead, he pulled her into a hug.

"Thanks for coming," he whispered in her ear.

They stood together for a moment. Linda liked the solid feel of him next to her. "I'm glad I could be here."

And then, before she knew it, Linda was outside and the reporters were talking to Duane.

It was Duane's moment. She could tell by the excited voices around that everyone was happy for him.

Linda went over to the café so she could sit in silence for a minute or two. She looked at the place on the wall where Duane's old guitar had been and she wondered if Lucy would add another memento from today to their collection of Jazz Man things.

Linda would never look at that guitar the same way again when she saw it hanging there on the wall.

And then it struck her. When Duane left this time, he'd likely take that guitar with him. And, since she'd seen his bus parked beside the café when she walked over, he'd probably be leaving soon. He'd be more organized this time, though. She had a hollow feeling that when he left today, he wasn't going to leave anything behind and certainly not that guitar. He loved that guitar. He'd only come here for the press conference; he had no reason to come back. He'd take everything he cared about with him this time.

Linda sat down in one of the chairs by the window. She'd known all along that Duane would leave again. He'd never pretended anything else.

She let herself breathe for a few minutes. Then she decided. She would do things differently this time. She wasn't going to be a coward and say goodbye in a note. She was going to be here to see him off. She'd smile and wish him a good life. She was going to be a friend and wave as that bus pulled out of town.

Linda stood up and walked closer to the café window. Boots was lying under the bus. The dog knew something was going to happen, too.

Duane saw Linda in the café when he left the church. The press conference had gone well. Half of the questions from the reporters were about recipes anyway. The other half were about his new faith. Duane had told the men he didn't have any experience in cooking or in being a Christian, but that he was going to learn. Phil passed out his last press release and everything was done. Duane and Phil had moved their suitcases to the bus earlier this morning. All that was left was to talk to Linda.

Duane didn't want to presume too much when it

came to Linda. When he saw her watching him from the window, though, he started to have hope. He walked up the café steps and opened the door.

"Thank you again for coming to church," Duane said as he stood inside the door with his guitar looped around his shoulder. "I know you're probably still not feeling well and I appreciate it."

He shifted his feet and she kept looking at him.

"You're leaving now, aren't you?" she asked.

Duane nodded. "I'm planning to write to you, though, and I'm hoping you'll answer me."

"Sure," Linda said with a blink. "That would be nice."

Nice isn't what Duane hoped for. Linda didn't look as if she understood what he was saying. "I mean, I want to be sure we keep in touch."

Linda gave him a tight smile. "Of course. Have a nice trip back."

Duane walked over to the wall where his guitar had hung until he'd unhooked it this morning. He took it off his shoulder and hung it on the wall hooks again.

"You're not taking your guitar?"

Duane shrugged. "I don't want it to get damaged in the move."

"I'll keep it safe for you." Linda finally had a glimmer of a smile on her face.

"Maybe your customers will enjoy seeing it on the wall."

Linda nodded.

Duane couldn't think of anything else to say.

He didn't want to leave, but he couldn't say that.

"You need to get someone to help you in the café, you know. Everyone gets sick sometimes."

Linda nodded. "Lucy helps if she's not in school."

"I could come and work the next time you're sick," Duane offered.

Linda looked at him funny. "It's a long way from Hollywood to Dry Creek."

Duane took a deep breath. "I don't think I'll be in Hollywood for long. I plan to settle in a small town somewhere around here. Maybe Idaho."

Linda's breath caught. "Why Idaho?"

"It's a lot like here."

"Then why not here?"

Linda wasn't looking at his eyes, so Duane wasn't sure if she meant anything by her words.

"A man has to go where he's welcome," Duane finally said at the same time that he heard a sharp bark outside. "Excuse me, that must be Boots."

Boots hardly ever barked. Duane walked over to the window and looked out. The old men were all gathered around the door to the bus. He supposed one of them was worried about it being stolen property.

"I'll come back," Duane said as he headed toward the door. He needed to sit Linda down and have a long talk with her. "Just let me be sure Boots is okay."

Linda nodded as Duane stepped out the door. She had made her pledge to say her goodbyes to him without bitterness and undue sorrow. But she wasn't going to be able to do it. She knew she couldn't do it the minute he talked about settling down somewhere else. She'd made her peace with losing Duane to Hollywood. But she wasn't ready to lose him to some Dry Creek look-alike town in Idaho.

Linda put her jacket back on and walked out of the café. She could hear the murmurs of the men from the porch, but she couldn't make out what was being said. Voices were being raised, though, and that didn't sound good.

Linda wrapped her arms around herself so she'd stay warm and walked over to the door of the bus. Elmer was talking.

"No," the older man was saying to Duane. "I insist on giving you the spare key. You just take that Cadillac out for a spin anytime you feel like it. Boys like cars like that."

Elmer held out a chain with a key on it.

"I'm not going to take your key or your car," Duane said. He was standing in front of the bus doors with his arms crossed. "And I'm not a boy anymore."

Linda could tell the second Duane saw her. He started walking over to her.

"You shouldn't be out here in this cold," Duane said to her.

He looked down at her and smiled.

"I'm okay." She didn't want to miss a second of the final minutes with Duane, but she was beginning to think he was going to kiss her right here in front of everyone. That would never do. Not with all of the grandfathers here.

"What Elmer means—" Charley stepped closer to them "—is that our cars are only machines."

"A Cadillac is more than a machine." Duane turned

and protested to Charley. "And no one needs to worry about me stealing anything."

Linda knew Duane had never been a thief. He had his problems growing up, but she'd always known he would never take what belonged to someone else.

It was chilly and everyone's face was flushed, but Charley's face went a brighter pink while Elmer started looking at his shoes.

"We know you're not a thief," Charley finally muttered. "That's what we're trying to say."

Duane looked at Linda for an explanation and she didn't have one. She shrugged.

Then Duane looked at the old men. "I don't have a clue what you're trying to say. But it doesn't matter. I'm going to take Linda inside the café before she gets any colder."

Duane wished he'd learned to ignore these old men when he was a kid. It would have made his life easier if he had just given up on trying to fit in with them and their town. Duane put his arm around Linda's shoulder. She didn't need to get chilled. He turned her around and started back to the café. He liked the feel of having her walking beside him.

"We're apologizing," Elmer finally shouted after them. "That's what we're saying. We're saying we're sorry we didn't treat you right."

Duane stopped in midstride and turned back. "You're the ones who asked the sheriff to check on me, aren't you?"

All three of the men hung their heads and nodded.

"So you're the ones who don't trust me?" Duane walked back. He shouldn't be surprised.

Charley looked up as Duane got there.

"Well, we trust you now," Charley said.

Duane grunted. He eyed the old men. He wasn't the skinny eleven-year-old who had come to town years ago. He was a man now. He was surprised he'd even considered letting these old men push him around.

"How much exactly do you trust me?" Duane asked. Linda was standing beside him and he put his arm around her again, hugging her close to his side. He expected them to bristle at that, but they didn't. Although, they did keep looking at him.

"I offered to lend you my Cadillac," Elmer finally said indignantly. "That's how much we trust you."

"I'll give you the keys to my car, too," Burt offered. "It needs a new carburetor so it's not working yet, but it will be."

Charley reached in his pocket and brought out his key chain. He just held it out.

"I don't need another car to drive," Duane said and shook his head. "I've got that bus."

All of the men turned and looked at the bus.

"You're packed up," Charley finally said.

Duane nodded. "I was going to head out now that church is over, but—"

"We have evening services tonight," Elmer offered. "Maybe you could stay for that."

Duane was so surprised at the offer that he forgot to tell them he was staying no matter what they thought.

"Thanks," Duane finally said.

"Everyone will miss you if you go." Charley stared at his feet.

"I doubt that," Duane said. He almost preferred these

men when they were calling the sheriff on him. At least then they didn't look so miserable.

Elmer looked up. "It's the gospel truth."

"You're welcome anytime in Dry Creek," Charley said.

Duane looked each of the three old men in the eye. "Just how welcome am I?"

"You're one of us," Charley said.

"No one else is more welcome," Burt added.

"You think I'd let just anyone drive that Cadillac of mine?" Elmer asked.

Duane saw no need to mention that he'd already decided to stay. A good negotiator knew not to tip his hand too soon. "Does that mean you would be okay if I stayed and dated Linda?"

Linda's smile turned to a grin. Duane turned to look at her.

Charley cleared his throat. "That would be acceptable to us. Very acceptable."

"That Enger place needs someone to live in it," Elmer said. "And it'd be good for a family, too, if—I mean after the dating—"

Duane wasn't listening any longer. All he saw was the look on Linda's face. He bent his head to kiss her.

"Germs," Linda squeaked.

Duane scarcely moved his lips away from her. "I can't let that stop me. Not now that I have everyone's approval."

Linda sighed. "Finally."

Duane wasn't sure if she was talking about the grandfathers or the kiss. Just to be on the safe side, he kissed her again.

Epilogue

It was late that summer when Duane Enger and Linda Morgan got married. They had to hire a dozen security guards to keep the reporters away from the Dry Creek church. Duane had left the band and started recording jazz in a studio he'd built in his great-aunt's barn. He didn't have the fame that the rock band had these days, but he was happy because he had a life now and could spend most of his time in Dry Creek. He'd decided to record in his studio and, outside of that, to only play a few concerts each year. He was gathering a whole new set of fans and he was still popular enough that the reporters wanted pictures of his wedding.

Phil was managing the press for the event.

Duane had told Linda to plan the wedding however she wanted it to be with no thoughts to the fans. If she wanted to dazzle people with a designer gown from Paris, he'd buy her one. If she wanted to do something simpler, he would be happy with that.

Linda decided to wear her mother's old wedding

dress. It was an ivory sheath with lace netting. She wanted to wear a dress that would match the era of the car they were driving away from the wedding ceremony.

Elmer had insisted they use his white Cadillac for the big day. He'd buffed it until it gleamed. He'd even had the leather upholstery repaired and had the wheels shined. As the guests arrived, it was standing in front of the church with a cascade of red roses covering part of its hood.

Linda knew all of this because her bridesmaid, Lucy, kept looking out the window of the back prayer room and telling her.

"Are you all ready?" Linda asked her sister. "You have your earrings?"

They had used the prayer room to dress in their wedding clothes.

"Of course."

Linda looked at the clock. There were five minutes left until she was scheduled to walk down the aisle. She'd waited so long to marry her high school sweetheart that she was surprised at how slow the final minutes seemed.

"I hear the pianist," Lucy finally said. "I think it's time."

Lucy walked over to her sister and gave her a quick hug before pulling the veil down so it covered her face.

"Here." Lucy handed Linda the bouquet of red roses.

Linda nodded. Her toes were cold. And her fingers. She took a deep breath.

The two sisters walked to the door of the prayer room and opened it. From there they could see the four honorary grandparents who were giving Linda away.

The honor of giving Linda away to Duane had been hotly debated for weeks in the café. At one point the grandfathers decided the only gentlemanly thing to do was to give the honor to Mrs. Hargrove since they could not agree on a representative. It was Linda who suggested all four of them give her away. The three men wore tuxedoes and Mrs. Hargrove wore a long lilac dress. Elmer and Burt had agreed to walk in front of Linda and Mrs. Hargrove and Charley were going to walk on each side of her.

Linda knew she was supposed to walk slowly, but when the wedding march started she leaned forward and whispered to Elmer and Burt. They obligingly walked a little faster.

Linda barely heard the music as she finally stood beside Duane. He reached out to take her hand and his hand was trembling. She had to blink.

The words Pastor Curtis said went by fast. Linda just kept holding Duane's hand.

"Now, I pronounce you husband and wife," the pastor said with a grin to Duane. "You may kiss your sweetheart."

The church erupted into applause, but Linda still heard Duane whisper that he loved her just before he bent his head to kiss her.

* * * * *

Dear Reader,

If you're like me, you don't always understand God's timing on things. In fact, sometimes it seems everything is way off. That's one of the things I wanted to highlight in this book. Linda had been determined to run off and be with her love, Duane, as he followed his music career. But then her mother died and Linda knew she needed to raise her younger sister. Linda was at a crossroads and it didn't seem as if God was being fair to make her choose. But there was only one choice she could make. She chose her duty to her little sister.

I'm sure you've faced situations like Linda's, when duty called you to do something that meant you had to give up something else you wanted to do. When this happens to me, I often think back to the verse in Romans 8:28, "…all things work together for good to them that love God, to them who are the called according to His purpose."

This doesn't mean all things work out the way we want them to. Living a life of faith often involves living a life of patience and waiting. As you read *Dry Creek Sweethearts,* I hope it encourages you in your life of faith.

I love to hear from my readers. If you get a chance, go to my Web site at www.JanetTronstad.com and you can send me an e-mail. If you don't have e-mail access, you can always drop me a note in care of the editors at Steeple Hill Books, 233 Broadway, Suite 1001, New York, NY 10279.

Yours,
Janet Tronstad

QUESTIONS FOR DISCUSSION

1. At the end of the book, how did you feel about the choice Linda made to stay in Dry Creek instead of going on the road with Duane in his music career? Have you ever faced a choice like this?

2. How do you think Linda saw God when she first made the choice to stay in Dry Creek? Do you think she would have said that He had a plan for her life and everything would be okay?

3. How do you think Linda saw God's hand in her life by the end of the book?

4. Linda and her sister felt as if they had many grandparents in Dry Creek. Do you have someone like that in your life? Are you someone like that in the life of someone else?

5. What do you think the church should be doing for young people, like Linda and her sister, who have no family? What does your church do?

6. At the beginning of the book, Linda did not really want any reminders of Duane in her café. Why do you think she let the guitar hang there?

7. Think of the past disappointments in your own life. Do you have reminders of them hanging around? Do those reminders serve any purpose for you now?

8. Do you think the grandparents in Linda's life were right in trying to protect her from Duane's presence? What would you have done in their place?

9. Were the older men in Dry Creek wise to be suspicious of Duane when he first stepped off the bus as a boy? They had heard rumors, and Duane looked tough. What would you do if a boy like that moved to a small town you lived in?

10. Was Lance a good friend to Duane? Did you have friends who didn't understand you when you became a Christian?

11. Lucy felt bad when she heard that she was the reason Linda had not been able to go away with Duane years ago. Have you ever had someone sacrifice something on your behalf? What did it feel like?

12. Why do you think Duane ended up singing "Jesus Loves Me" when his musical talent would have let him sing a more sophisticated song?

Look for Charley and
Mrs. Hargrove's story
A DRY CREEK COURTSHIP
Available in September
From Love Inspired

Love Inspired
HISTORICAL
INSPIRATIONAL HISTORICAL ROMANCE

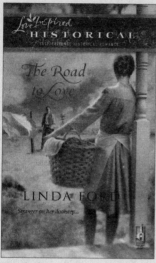

The Long Way Home

In the depths of the Depression, young widow Kate Bradshaw was struggling to hold on to the family farm and raise two small children. She had only her faith to sustain her—until the day drifter Hatcher Jones came walking up that long, lonely road. She longed to make him see that all his wandering had brought him home at last.

Look for

The Road
to Love

by

LINDA FORD

Available May wherever books are sold.

www.SteepleHill.com

Steeple
Hill®

LIH82787

REQUEST YOUR FREE BOOKS!

2 FREE INSPIRATIONAL NOVELS
PLUS 2
FREE
MYSTERY GIFTS

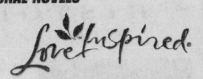

YES! Please send me 2 FREE Love Inspired® novels and my 2 FREE mystery gifts (gifts are worth about $10). After receiving them, if I don't wish to receive any more books, I can return the shipping statement marked "cancel". If I don't cancel, I will receive 4 brand-new novels every month and be billed just $4.24 per book in the U.S. or $4.74 per book in Canada, plus 25¢ shipping and handling per book and applicable taxes, if any*. That's a savings of over 20% off the cover price! I understand that accepting the 2 free books and gifts places me under no obligation to buy anything. I can always return a shipment and cancel at any time. Even if I never buy another book, the two free books and gifts are mine to keep forever.

113 IDN ERXA 313 IDN ERWX

Name	(PLEASE PRINT)	
Address		Apt. #
City	State/Prov.	Zip/Postal Code

Signature (if under 18, a parent or guardian must sign)

Order online at www.LoveInspiredBooks.com
Or mail to Steeple Hill Reader Service:
IN U.S.A.: P.O. Box 1867, Buffalo, NY 14240-1867
IN CANADA: P.O. Box 609, Fort Erie, Ontario L2A 5X3
Not valid to current subscribers of Love Inspired books.

Want to try two free books from another series?
Call 1-800-873-8635 or visit www.morefreebooks.com

* Terms and prices subject to change without notice. N.Y. residents add applicable sales tax. Canadian residents will be charged applicable provincial taxes and GST. This offer is limited to one order per household. All orders subject to approval. Credit or debit balances in a customer's account(s) may be offset by any other outstanding balance owed by or to the customer. Please allow 4 to 6 weeks for delivery. Offer available while quantities last.

LIREG08

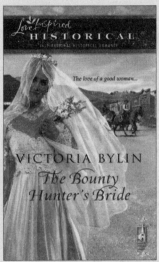

TITLES AVAILABLE NEXT MONTH

Don't miss these four stories in May

TO LOVE AGAIN by Bonnie K. Winn
A Rosewood, Texas novel

Laura Manning moved her family to Rosewood to take over her late husband's share of a real-estate firm. Who was Paul Russell to tell her she couldn't? She'd prove to the handsome Texan that she could do anything.

A SOLDIER'S HEART by Marta Perry
The Flanagans

After wounded army officer Luke Marino was sent home, he refused physical therapy. But Mary Kate Flanagan Donnelly needed Luke's case to prove herself a capable therapist. If only it wasn't so hard to keep matters strictly business...

MOM IN THE MIDDLE by Mae Nunn
Texas Treasures

Juggling caring for her son and elderly parents kept widow Abby Cramer busy. Then her mother broke her hip at a store. Good thing store employee Guy Hardy rushed in to save the day with his tender kindness toward her whole family—especially Abby herself.

HOME SWEET TEXAS by Sharon Gillenwater

When a strange man appeared to her like a mirage in the desert, he was the answer to the lost and injured woman's prayers. But she couldn't tell her handsome rescuer, Jake Trayner, who she was. Because she couldn't remember....

LICNM0408